page seventeen

issue twelve

edited by

beau hillier

First published by Busybird Publishing 2015

ISBN 978-0-9944838-5-0

ISSN 1832 5416

Cover image: Martin Nitschke
Cover design: Busybird Publishing
Layout and typesetting: Robert Frolla at Busybird Publishing
Chief Editor: Beau Hillier
Editors: Stephanie Heriot, Kristin Pedder, Ashley Tarleton
Proofreaders: Rebecca Courtney, Belle Savage

Busybird Publishing
PO Box 855
Eltham Victoria
Australia 3095
www.busybird.com.au

Email:pageseventeen@busybird.com.au
Facebook: Page Seventeen Literary Magazine
Twitter: @p17mag

Contents

Foreword

I wonder if anyone reads forewords anymore.

I voted for Tony Abbott.*

With that off my chest, back to business.

Page seventeen has had a big journey. These days, a literary journal making it past Issue 10 is not a small thing. Now we're at Issue 12, and for the occasion *page seventeen* has completed its transition to having a digital presence. Makes sense, when considering that our mission statement is to provide a home for new writers, and give them a platform to gain a publication credit and exhibit their work. We can wax lyrical for lifetimes about the positives and negatives of the internet's influence on the publishing industry, but for emerging writers it's a valuable medium. One that P17 might be able to take advantage of to spread the names of this issue's contributors a little bit further.

As always I have my thank-yous, because putting an issue of *page seventeen* together is not a lone-wolf exercise. The P17 editorial committee – particularly Kristin Pedder, Stephanie Heriot and Ashley Tarleton – have been essential in putting the latest issue together. And as always a big thanks to the team at the heart of Busybird Publishing – Blaise van Hecke, Kev Howlett, Les Zigomanis and Melissa Cleeman – for their support and backing not just for this issue, but for *page seventeen* in general since Issue 9.

Also, I need to take a selfish moment and thank my fiancé Belinda for all her support while I've been working on P17. I'll be the first to admit I get obsessive about work. That she both puts up with it and continues to express her support is a combination that I do not take for granted.

Does any more really need to be said? We have a juicy new issue of *page seventeen* to share. Let's enjoy it.

Beau Hillier | Editor, *page seventeen*

*Of course I didn't – who would admit to it now anyway? – but hey, maybe it got your attention.

Competition Results

Short Story

Winner:	'Rooms without doors' by Willa Hogarth
Runner-Up:	'Louis' by Edie Mitsuda
Shortlisted:	'Cold currents' by Susi Fox
	'Ships of the desert' by Carmel Lillis
	'Macalister' by Paul Mill

Poetry

Winner:	'Alice and Edward' by Janine McGinness-Whyte
Runner-Up:	'The glass reverie' by Virginia Danahay
Shortlisted:	'Oral sex' by Judith A Green
	'Ironing' by Jenny Macaulay
	'In defence of the bodhran' by Leonie Needham
	'Beginning with a given line' by Rodney Williams

Wish

Sarah Andrews

Alone, I stand outside the Artful Dodger's studio – a small building with graffiti spray-painted around it. All I know about this place is that it is owned by the Jesuits and that it is a place where troubled youth can create art. I cringe at the idea of religion combined with troubled youth, and wonder about the Jesuits' underlying motives. I think of my studies, of philosophy and Nietzsche, of how even a martyr has self-serving needs. I wonder, do these people work on unconscious levels to please themselves?

Inside the small gallery stands a skinny teenage girl with blonde hair. I lean against the glass door and ask for Mary, the administrator.

'Watch the door,' says the girl. It is decorated with stencils and streamers.

I feel strangely vulnerable, yet I am unsure of why. Is it the hangover I am feeling from last night? Murky, like the drugs I was on when I had my gallbladder out.

'Fair, fat and forty, that's what they say,' I said at the time.

'Not necessarily,' said the surgeon.

An older lady with a warm round face greets me, and leads me through a computer lab surrounded by artwork. In Mary's tiny back office she is eating nuts and wipes the crumbs from her mouth. Middle-aged, she wears a floral dress and long earrings. She has the colourful community services look down pat. She seems overly professional in her demeanour.

'So you're here to be immersed. What class is this for?'

'Non-fiction. It really shouldn't take long.'

Mary leads me through the studios. We weave amongst an influx of visitors, teachers and students. Through graphic design spaces and an art room with hanging mobiles, so fast I have no time to appreciate anything. I decide that I really don't like her. She is overly efficient.

In the art room, Mary tells me about talks of dual issues. I learn that the teenagers have mental health problems as well as drug problems. The mental health organisations don't deal with the ones who have drug problems, and the drug rehabs don't deal with the ones who have mental health problems. Mary explains that, in many ways, these teenagers fend for themselves. Once trust is built between a worker and artist, the worker can refer the youth to a housing organisation. The waiting lists are long, though, and only add anxiety and a sense of desperation.

In the exhibition room she stops talking. I notice the giant wishing well. It is surrounded by bricks and I stare into the bottom. Convoluted pastel slides move underneath the water. Looking at the wishing well I can't make out what the multimedia pictures mean. I think of the teenage girl who created it; I wonder what she might have been wishing for.

Mary moves me on again, into the music studio. The orange lighting illuminates interesting murals and equipment. I reveal how I went to a community school as a teenager. Our band room was very similar. I played the keyboard. We were tight and we were good. We played for other schools in their gymnasiums. The room would bang their heads along to the music. We felt famous.

Mary asks me to have a seat on a narrow couch. We sit side by side but maintain distance. She begins in her tour guide voice again, telling me how the Killing Heidi guitarist runs the music room; how there are lots of volunteers from the art world who work here; how two local teenagers, Fablice and 'Gstorm', have won 'Best Australian Hip Hop Artist of the Year'. Fablice was a child soldier in Africa. She tells me of an aunty and niece getting cancer and I interject, perhaps becoming too immersed in her martyrdom.

'But how do you separate yourself from this place? How do you feel when you go home?'

Mary draws back a breath. 'I love it. It's about coming together with positive ideas and learning from others. These teenagers are an inspiration, they aren't sad.'

I still feel overly empathetic. I would never be able to work in a place like this.

When I was seventeen, my thirteen year old sister and I had to find somewhere to live due to a family breakdown because of the death of my father. We rented a dual occupancy in Brunswick at the back of a doctor's surgery. It had an old but stable collection of rooms. It had big windows. We looked after each other. Good Shepherd Family Services paid us two hundred and fifty dollars a week tax-free. I waitressed six days a week, cash in hand. I still collected Centrelink payments. We had a supermarket next door to us and our small fridge was overflowing. We had hummus and Vienna bread for our breakfasts. We had furniture, a lush backyard and an Irish wolfhound. We lived in this place in Brunswick over twenty years ago. I often consider how much has changed in regards to rental housing, the obscene cost of it nowadays. The Artful Dodger's teenagers are mainly couch-surfing.

Mary tells me that no-one working at this space is religious at present. I feel I would like to get to know her. I wonder why I dislike so many people when I first meet them. I tell her how I now live in co-operative housing; she nods.

'That is great, lucky for you!' She is not sarcastic.

On our way to the art cupboard a large teenage boy is laying on a couch, with a teenage girl comforting him. The stillness of his limbs and the terror around his eyes reveals a mental agony.

Mary explains to them that I am a writing student.

'Hi, nice night,' I say.

They look at me with emptiness.

Mary hands me magazines, CDs and books from the art cupboard. On the way out I knock over a cup of pins. Mary rescues most of them from the floor. The tour is over.

My sister always listened to better bands than me, more underground ones. Her creative image later allowed her to fit easily into scenes. I only looked cool in my mid-teens. Skinny, fitting into my mother's vintage outfits perfectly. When my sister lived with me in Brunswick, I would squander a lot of the Good Shepherd money on beer and dope. As an adult, she reminds me of this. Writing these days requires new levels of responsibility. Sometimes I can almost feel the changes happening about me.

I stand in the space, surrounded by an overflow of teenagers. I look at the art and then walk to the spinach pizzas. I take two. I have an insatiable hunger. A worker offers me a drink. Has she been counting the pizzas?

I stare again at the well that would look great in my lounge room. I look at a rusty knife on the wall crossed over an axe. Is that what the tools are called? My head spins with words as the room crowds. I forget what the teenage solo artist looks like.

'Are you an artist?' I ask a girl with brown hair standing next to me.

'No.'

I remember friends from my community high school. A diverse range of students, mostly from low socio-economic backgrounds, some with a diagnosis. We were all close and knew each others' houses, and whose parents would not be home on what days. We never felt sad for each other, only comparing trivial things like our Nike runners. I think I have had it too easy.

I look around the room of young people. There is a girl dressed in blue – blue make-up and blue hair. They are busy chatting and laughing to one another. They are not going to talk to me.

'Typical artists,' I think, and leave through the glass door, past a lean man in the dark. I catch his leftover cigarette smoke in my throat.

How a schizophrenic hears

Bee Williamson

My vision-impaired friend discusses in her blog, At the Gateway to Blindness, what it is like to experience sensory loss. So I thought people might like to know how this one schizophrenic hears.

A while ago Andrew Denton was given the opportunity to experience hearing voices first-hand in his documentary 'Angels and Demons' as part of his *Enough Rope* series on the ABC. He was handed a CD walkman and headphones and given a few hours to experience what it was like to hear voices. He didn't say exactly what he heard, but he did say it was mostly slinging, stinging insults and commands.

Although I can't speak for everyone, the simplicity of the program's approach did make me want to stand up and explain hearing voices from first-hand experience.

Firstly, voices are directional – not some amorphous blob of sound. So that means the sound appears to come from above or below me, or in front or behind me. It is clear enough to say it is either male or female, adult or child, very young or very old. It is exactly like someone is standing in the room talking to you; the only difference is you can't see them. Believe it or not, I can even sometimes smell them! Particularly if they have been drinking, smoking marijuana or have recently died.

There is nothing 'dreamy' about hearing voices for me. They are directional, with specific age, sex and nationality. Sometimes they even have accents. There is a difference as to whether they are, for example, inside or outside my home, as well as – and this is a big difference – whether the voices are coming from inside or outside my head. Inside my head is better, being less abrasive than external voices.

I also hear my thoughts 'broadcast'; mixed with the voices, this is hugely distressing. 'Thought broadcasting' is a psychotic feature of schizophrenia and developed in me during the years since my breakdown. I suppose you could say it is like an external row between my thoughts and the voices 'broadcast' wherever I go.

It means I can't go to music festivals or big parties – the white noise is far too hard. But so are Fed Square's huge screens and the Arts Centre theatres and concert halls, all with lots of this noise.

The voices are mostly distinguishable from my own thoughts and the conversations going on around me. It's like when you're talking to someone in a café, you can tell the difference between your thoughts and your friends' words. I suppose you could say it is just an 'internal conversation'.

A psychic once said to me that I hear voices because I have so much to say and so much desire for conversation. Ha!

I have seen ghosts only a few times in my life. Hearing voices is not like seeing ghosts. But unfortunately this does not mean I can't feel them. I spend most nights telling them to leave, while they imitate insect bites on my legs, just for fun, always when I am just about to drop off. I have felt slices, pokes, stabs and hits; I have received death threats, anger and retribution.

These voices are very real. They are not like a tape being played over and over. They usually refer to specific people, objects, events or thoughts. They are specific to the situation you are in, and the person and place you are in. Mine are not some jumble of words slung at me. They are precisely relevant to what I'm trying to do in my day. I'm a designer, poet and artist so I usually find reprieve in work – to focus all your mind on something specific for just a few hours at a time is a wonderful rest.

Until I befriended my voices they were very hostile. Some would help, some would hinder, and some would seek to destroy. But now, a lot of what I hear is a great help. There are just a few unhappy souls that are stuck and enjoy taunting me with unexpected pain.

I want to reiterate, the voices are not just some jumble of words. They are specific to what you are seeing, hearing, smelling, tasting. They show every emotion and tone an adult would show. They are not monotonous, especially now I have befriended them. They focus on and show every detail you are seeking to understand – while out at a gallery, at a shop or on the web. They are quiet when they've had their say, but can be vindictive when not acknowledged.

I guess what I'm trying to get across is that voices aren't just random utterances of robots in the cellular level of the brain. Research shows our brains light up in the recognition-of-speech area of the brain when we hear voices; hearing the voice of an invisible stranger is no different from hearing the voice of my mother next to me.

One big change, as a spark ignites the bonfire, is befriending my voices. I had spent an age shouting, swearing and voicelessly turning my back to the beings that besiege my life. Around 2005 I began to listen – just listen. With no fight left, I let them into my world. Then? They became my friends.

Even now I fight, but only the bad ones. The good ones, my invisible ones, began to help me work. They helped by igniting the fire in dreams – which began a series of photographs that were exhibited around my hometown in cafes and galleries. So a close relationship began with creativity … they would finish the lines of my poems and tell me when to put the brush down on a painting. They heightened the mood while listening to music, to lead me to dance to Cuban salsa, and just … let … go.

Mad or not, there is nothing wrong in dancing by yourself to Alicia Keys or the Black Eyed Peas and singing to the top of your vocal range on nights of bad TV. I don't care if that can't be understood by any fifty year old, because every fourteen year old will know the sanctity of the hairbrush and the shiny wooden boards, each beckoning. You don't have to be mad to feel it; just think of the movie *Ghost* and you've got the story.

What was a tooth and nail fight for survival and a terrible state of affairs became a wondrous life of love affairs – for an invisible man is not a man without power, and he showed me that love is possible, even in spirit. What was an enemy can become an ally, what is a monster can become a kind man, and what is a curse can become creativity.

Alice and Edward
Janine McGinness-Whyte

Love branches, a living cell divides,
a sapling, bending to breeze or need;
a heart regenerates and grows
a dedicated corner for each made dear.
Capacity extends, so ardour widens,
concepts of marriage and union
are worked like an autumn field –
the furrows in our brows deepening.
The inevitable falling, into another;
an inseparable hue, penetrates skin,
I with you, you with me –
a desert of separation between.
A rotating world scarcely notices,
intimate hours stolen, golden;
an embrace worth more than reputation,
we watch a star burning.
Yet time has a tally, and calls;
your light now leaving, ascends
while I am tethered to body
and desolate earth without sense.
With each breath, I empty,
having lost all hunger, all hope;
sheet of sky, bleached of colour,
and I am blank with misery.

Room without doors
Willa Hogarth

It's the colour of Matt's blood that hits her first. A deep crimson – rich and vibrant, the colour of life. It spurts like water from an underground bore. A nauseous feeling swamps her as she stares at his severed left arm dangling from the shaft connecting tractor and post-hole digger. It hangs like washing out to dry, a distinct line above his elbow where his rolled-up shirt stops – white above and below, the skin burnt chocolate-brown. The caw of a crow. Sarah glares at the bird. Will it beat her to the arm?

His body lies in a pool of blood seeping into the dry dust and manure stirred by years of milling sheep. His chest rises and falls with a shallow breath, his tanned face ashen. Half-closed eyes give him a relaxed look. Shep lies beside him, Matt's hand on the dog's head. When Matt's eyes focus on her she pulls her shoulders back and clenches her jaw.

He points at the post-hole digger still being driven by the shaft connected to the tractor, spearing its auger into the earth with an embarrassed whine as if wanting to stop and be forgiven. She jumps onto the tractor, depresses the clutch and yanks down the lever; the shaft stops turning and the digger gives a relieved sigh. Then she turns the key to off. Silence. The sheep yards empty, the smell of fresh soil beside newly dug holes, a pile of fence poles waiting. Her knees throw up a spray of dust when she hits the ground beside him, pushing Shep out of the way. She grips his arm and shakes it.

'What happened?'

'Guard was off,' he says, forcing out words. 'Shirt caught in the shaft.' His eyes close. Sarah's hand covers her mouth, her heart flutters. God. How long does she have? She rips off her jacket. Places it around the stump. Blood seeps through, the dark stain spreading.

'Hang in, Matt. I'll ring the air ambulance.' No response. The severed arm looks like a bizarre sculpture, fingers bent as if holding a cricket ball. She initially falters but then runs over and grips it hard and forces the cogs to let go; she races back to the house not letting her eyes glance at the surreal image in her hands. At the fridge she drags out ice-cream and frozen meat and pushes the arm into the freezer, bending the elbow to make it fit. She shoves the door to make it close. Is she really doing this?

On the phone, The Flying Doctor Service immediately throws questions at her.

'Just get here. Now!'

'Sorry, love, we have to get the details.' They tell her the plane will be forty minutes.

'That's too long!' She slams the phone down. Dragging a sheet out of the linen cupboard, she tears strips off, folds the rest into a pressure pad and dashes back to the sheep yards.

Shep is licking the blood lying in small pools in the dust beside Matt. 'Get out!' She kicks the dog. He yelps. Matt is now lying still, eyes closed, face paler than before. She puts a finger under his nostrils and feels spurts of air; presses the pad against the stump and awkwardly bandages the torn-off strips around it.

A glance in the direction the plane will come. She should have checked on him when he was late for lunch. Thumbs and fingers squeeze her crossed arms until they hurt. At last. A drone. The plane lands on the airstrip beside the yards, doctor and flight nurse hurrying over with a stretcher. After a professional glance at Matt, the doctor's smile changes to a straight line sending a shiver through her body. They lift Matt onto the stretcher, carry him to the plane, insert a drip, apply dressings. The plane roars.

Sitting beside him, she hits her forehead with a fist. 'His arm. It's still in the fridge.'

The doctor shakes his head.

***

It's oppressively humid – like a rain cloud has snuck into the bank building and is drowning them both. Customers and staff glance through the glass-walled office at her and John Eastlake, the manager.

'Anna, I'm so sorry about your husband. Such a shock. Anything we can do …'

Yes. Help her keep the station going. 'Thanks John. I appreciate that.' She stares at the thin lips that will tell her yes or no. She watches him slide a hand up to his face to pull a red bulbous nose – a carrot in the middle of sandy soil. Alcohol, they say. He clears his throat.

'Now, this loan application.' His pen taps the form.

She makes herself tall and takes a deep breath. 'I'll only need it till the drought breaks.' Her friend Jill works in the bank and has told her the best spiel to use – how she's always done the station books and still has Mick, their station hand, to help. She finishes with a tear jerker, '… and I know Matt would want me to keep the place going.' It's true.

She remembers their instant attraction – meeting the bushie from Bourke on the Mosman ferry going home from work. 'Marry me and come and live in poverty in the bush,' he said after six months of visits and lengthy phone calls. She left the city in a flash. And she adapted: set up a computerised system for keeping station records, created a garden, redecorated the house, made friends with tough local women.

She shivers, feeling Matt's work-calloused hands stroking her back, seeing his muscular body – white except for sunburnt forearms and an eccentric vee at the neck, places where the sun bites.

Mr Eastlake looks down, massaging his nose again. 'I know you've done a terrific job with the books. But, running the place?'

She clenches her bag. 'Mick's been there for ten years. Knows the place like the back of his hand.'

He clasps both hands in front of his mouth. 'Big responsibility. What was your job before?'

'Teacher.'

'Oh, right.' He nods. 'Thought of selling and …?'

She pictures life in Sydney – standing in front of a class of defiant teenagers; searching for a unit to rent; vile air, snarling traffic and acres of asphalt. 'Don't you think a woman can run a sheep station?'

His shifts in his chair. 'Yes. Of course. I … I'm just concerned that …'

'No way I'm selling.' She shakes her head, pushing away the image of people walking through the graceful but seen-better-days homestead and raising an eyebrow at the battered electric stove and torn curtains. 'I'll make a go of it.'

He shrugs. 'A burly son would help.'

Tears try to force their way out. 'That's true.' A shaky voice. The morning before it happened there were raised voices and sharp feelings. About kids. Again.

'Anna, you're thirty-four!'

'For Christ's sake, IVF costs money. Wait till the drought breaks.'

'You're a control freak. It'll be too late!' He strode out of the kitchen slamming the door, leaving her throwing dishes onto the rack.

'God, you're hopeless. You never think about money!'

***

The forty-kilometre drive home is so familiar it's like reading a story she knows well: clumps of dull-green mulga; two-toned dead trees, parts of the trunks blackened by fire and the rest bleached grey by the sun; and tired sheep, hollowed spaces behind their ribcages, trotting along, stopping to snatch a mouthful of dry creamy grass and continuing on as if they have an appointment to get to. She concentrates — there are potholes, wallabies bounding across the road in low dusk light, the bumpy diversion round a fallen gumtree.

Down the long hill and past the cluster of wattle trees beside the creek where they used to swim. They came here the week before he … She stops and walks over to the pool, the water level lower now from lack of rain. Remembers her body sliding through a tunnel of bubbles, feeling the power of her arms propelling her forward, hearing the underwater roar of splashing legs. His face above the wrinkles of mud-coloured water, wearing his life-is-good grin. It pulls her back to them, together. God, she loved that man.

Back home she'd cooked a mushroom omelette for lunch – it smelt so rich. A bottle of white wine, an afternoon in bed under the mosquito net. They were good in the sack. She woke to Matt's arm around her and the sun-stroked pattern of lace curtains on the bedroom wall. 'We'll have kids,' she said. 'I promise.'

A fish jumps out of the water and plops back. She swats a march fly biting her calf, smells heat bouncing off the rocks. She rips off her clothes and before the hot rocks burn her feet, makes a running dive. Swims like hell as if racing to beat her memories – over to the other bank and back, over and back. The top ten centimetres of water like a warm blanket, but icy cold underneath. She makes her body float, arms out, the warm water holding her, sun melting her face.

Standing beside the creek, she lets her body dry off – looks up to see a black snake moving determinedly through the water. Her hand goes to her chest. The snake slides onto the bank and disappears into the undergrowth of surrounding scrub; a dangerous red-bellied black. Her body shivers.

Opening the last gate before home, she feels the ache of her bruised heart. From here she sees the homestead Matt inherited – a rambling weatherboard house surrounded by trees and shrubs she planted eight years ago on arrival, now struggling in the drought. The vegetable garden now growing carrots with roots like noses as they struggle with brackish bore water. The background of messy sheds and sheep yards, piles of hay under canvas, trucks, the old tractor.

Mick stands beside the tool shed waiting, Shep next to him wagging his tail. The dog has immediately switched allegiance from Matt to Mick and barely looks at her.

'G'day, Mrs Martin. Got a minute?' He's never called her Anna in the whole eight years. She smiles at him through the car window.

'Sure thing, Mick. Shoot.'

Mick is the slow-moving, slow-to-smile, Aussie bush guy – the 'she'll-be-right' type she trusts. He takes one more puff of his roll-your-own, drops it on the ground and squashes it with the heel of his boot. He leans against the 4WD, one foot crossed over the other, one hand on his hip, staring at a spot just below her eyes. 'Think I told you the bore needs fixing. Can you get the pipes tomorrow?'

She feels her body crashing – into town again? 'Reckon you could get them?'

He looks away. 'Boss did that sort of thing.' Something fizzes between them like a fire cracker that's just been lit.

'Okay. Got the measurements?'

'The boss already did that. Reckon you'll find them on his desk.'

'Okay.' She'll never replace him, will she?

'There's a sale on Friday. Want me to get the ewes in?'

'What do you reckon? Good time to sell?'

He shrugs. 'Dunno. Your decision.'

She frowns and looks away. 'I'll think about it, Mick.'

***

Inside the house, she phones Jill. 'Don't know if I'll get the loan.'

'Anna, just keep up the broken record. You'll wear him down.'

She wants to tell her about Mick but her throat chokes. 'Can't talk. Ring you later.'

Sitting on the front verandah with a mug of strong milky tea, she watches Shep slink along the ground, ears crumpled, tongue hanging out like a pink ribbon, panting, pretending to be the lowest of the low.

'Why do you do that, you silly dog?' He creeps up the stairs to lick her hand and then slumps down beside her. An image of Matt on his motorbike with Shep balanced on the tray behind, both leaning over in unison as they take off to muster sheep. A pang in her chest. The dog has never obeyed her – only comes when he wants to. With Matt he was obedience personified, even though he kept the dog tied up. She never understood why people in the bush treated their sheep dogs like that.

'You can't molly-coddle them, Anna,' Matt said, shaking his head and laughing. 'You city slicker, you.'

Shep's unchained now. She strokes his head feeling the coarse hair; grips the loose skin on his back and holds it; slides her hand over his rib cage as it moves up and down and feels the warmth of his body. A sharp pain in her hand. Tooth marks. She slaps him hard and he slides away; scowls at his retreating back and strokes her hand. Damn him.

The loan. If Matt were there, he'd be shaking hands with John Eastlake – man-to-man. A successful deal. Matt. Gone. Out of her life. She glances down at Shep looking at her sideways from the bottom of the stairs. She thinks of John Eastlake's mouth. Mick's eyes not looking at her. 'Shit!' She stamps her foot. Shep jumps and slinks away.

***

Three days later she is driving back from town with pipes bumping around in the back, speeding like a racing driver. She dashes straight inside the house to dial Jill's number, and stands tapping her foot.

'Jill. I've got the loan.'

'That's great. Now at least you've got a choice.'

'Choice?' A pain in her chest.

'Stay or go back to Sydney … you know.'

She frowns. 'Got to go, Jillie. Someone's at the door.'

Mick stands on the steps holding a battered Akubra in his hands, his eyes looking at the usual spot. He tells her his brother needs him to work their cattle property way out west, how sorry he is about leaving her in the lurch. A red flush on his neck shows through the dark tan. She manages a smile.

'It's okay, Mick. I understand.'

The old chair on the verandah creaks when she leans back. She gulps hot tea, burning her lips. Damn Mick! Overhead, black cockatoos screech as they fly over desiccated country; there is a familiar hum of an escaping plane. She glances up and watches the silver streak flashing in sunlight. A ripple runs through her body. She plonks the tea down. Her shoulders drop; she starts rocking backwards and forwards, hands covering her face, chest shaking, tears sliding down her cheeks like rain on a windowpane. Big lumpy sobs. She's a blob of pain in a room without doors. She wants to set the table for two, feel the heat of his body beside her in bed, hear his words, 'What do you reckon, mate?' When her tears finally stop she wipes her face with a sleeve. She's shivering.

Leaning back, she stares at the landscape flooded with heat: brown earth and clumps of stunted trees all the way to the skyline and a brutal blue sky without a puff of cloud. She gazes at Shep lying in the dust, looking at her from under shrivelled trees. Imagines finding a new manager, more meetings with Mr Eastlake, dealing with shearing contractors, wool classers, truck drivers, stock and station agents. The assistant in the hardware store today – his helpful advice and look of concern, but then letting his eyes slide away.

She thinks of Sydney: diving through boisterous waves on early morning surfs; the warmth of her mother's arms, hands patting her back; sitting with big sis at the Oriental Bar on Pitt Street with a glass of white wine, fingers smearing her initials in the cool wetness of the glass.

In the distant sky she sees the plane, now barely visible, with a white thread trailing behind. Fleeing.

The glass reverie
Virginia Danahay

Summer fails to last
And the damp leaf smell of autumn
Brings finality to another night alone.
Memories in shards
Scratch away at my dreams.
When are you coming home?
Words impossible to speak
Seem easier to write, and easier to erase
So they're not left hanging, unbalanced in the air
As harsh and indelible as the city lights
You're lost in, somewhere.
While I'm here pretending to be poetic, to be rhythmic,
Delicate as Tennessee and yet
Thoughts, random and clumsy as children,
Clatter around my brain.
Where are you?
My company has sent you into a kindness of strangers.
Tom tells his sister to blow out her candles.
Their light flickers, then dies
And I'm left here in darkness, in loneliness
Feeling like Laura.
Hope, a tiny glass animal,
Shatters into pieces.

Louis
Edie Mitsuda

Louis climbs the stairs at the Wassaic train station, surrounded by a kind of pre-dawn darkness that is more grey than any other colour. The whole of New England has been frozen for days, and Louis makes a sharp, involuntary noise as he skids along an unseen patch of ice on the platform. His breath travels visibly in and out of his mouth like he's a sleepy winter dragon. He can hear the train pulling in behind him – Louis has truly mastered the art of arriving at the station in the exact nick of time. If you could call such a thing an art – really, it's just one of the more useful by-products of his ever-present laziness. Daybreak has been avoiding the world lately, and Louis can see an array of small lights still gently peppering the horizon, their sympathetic glow reminding him he's not the only person awake at this strange hour. Louis turns towards the train as the carriage doors slide open, grateful for the warm gust of air waiting for him at the entrance as though he is an old and distinguished friend.

***

It was his mother's suggestion for him to take the job in New York. Louis thought that a two-and-a-half hour commute each way was a terrible idea, but he was desperate, and desperate people listen to their mothers. He remembers that day vividly, her standing in their tiny living room, hands akimbo. *It's not like it'll be every day of the week, Louis. Think of the experience you'll be getting.* She waved the television remote at him. Think of the experience. Louis caught a whiff of New York City once when he was twenty-two, and thought it smelled like possibility and the type of melancholy all artists need to produce greatness. Louis knows this odour as something else now: urine, mainly, and the stink of other people's lives. Or maybe it's just that, without the girl around, nothing hopeful is what it seems any more. If anything Louis's mother was almost more distraught than he was when the girl left. Before marrying Louis's father, his mother was an Abramowicz, so it was nice to spend a few imagined Rosh Hashanahs cooking teiglach with her son's little Jewish girlfriend in her own little Jewish kitchen. Louis would sit and watch as the girl popped almonds into her rosebud mouth, one after another, and thought about how much he adored the women in his life. That was just about the best version of himself he can remember.

***

Pawling. This is Pawling, folks. The driver's voice is loud over the intercom, and he draws his vowels out in such a way that makes the ensuing silence more apparent than it should be. The walls of the train are beige, flecked with small blue dots, and Louis presses his forehead against one of the largest and most appealing dots hard enough to feel the grain of the plastic transferring onto his face. A lone woman files silently into the carriage and sits down opposite him. She loosens her coat and Louis swears he can feel the heat from her body hitting the side of his cheek.

'Cold out there today,' she says.

Louis tries inconspicuously to separate his forehead from where he'd just placed it.

'It is,' he replies. 'It feels kind of raw.' Louis smiles but is annoyed with the lady. Why would you enter into a conversation with somebody on a train? Now there's going to be an unspoken obligation hanging over them both for the rest of the journey, the air will be thick with it. Maybe he could sit in a different carriage once they transferred at Southeast.

'You going to New York?'

'Yeah,' Louis says. 'You?'

The woman nods and is silent for a while, but Louis can tell she wants to say more.

'My boyfriend's there,' she declares, eventually. 'Haven't seen him for a week.'

'Oh yeah, what does he do?'

'He's a fireman. A few guys got sick over at one of the Brooklyn stations so he was transferred out there.'

'I've heard there's something going around.' There is a pride in her voice that is making Louis feel terrible things.

'What're you doing when you get to New York?'

'Work,' he replies. 'I work there.'

She seems surprised. 'That's a long way, just for work.'

'I know. I think I'm going to quit.'

'What sort of work do you do?'

'I'm an intern at Amos Goldfinger's studio.' Louis pauses but the woman offers nothing so he continues. 'He's a sculptor. I don't know, famous probably isn't the right word to use here.'

'Well, with a name like Goldfinger he ought to be.' She laughs but Louis has heard that one before.

'I had a doctor called Goldfinger once,' Louis says. She laughs again and he joins her this time.

'So where are you from?'

'Housatonic,' he replies.

'God, that's even further away than I thought,' she says. 'Beautiful out there, though.'

'It is.' He can't think of anything else to say.

'The Housatonic River.'

Louis's about to reply but thinks better of it, unsure if that was a question or a statement or if it matters either way.

***

In reality, Louis spent some of his best days down by the Housatonic River. And even though the part by his house was really more the Williams River, nobody ever called it by either of those titles. He and the girl just named it 'the brook' and would sit for hours there, in the easiness of summer, feeling then that they were both people with kind and compatible hearts. The girl would tell him about how her pet rabbit was eaten by a snapping turtle at the other end of the brook, where it turned into the Housatonic River for real. She would say it was a sad incident without truly meaning it, because it happened so long ago. It was like another world down there, and they both felt it, a sort of significance they couldn't quite put their finger on. The Blue Jays and the maples all seemed to be participating in a sort of quiet drama written solely for those woods, the idle sky forming a perfect, wide backdrop. And the little river, the tenacity of it, babbling constantly and effervescently towards something greater than itself.

***

Southeast is possibly the most tedious part of Louis's morning commute. He doesn't like having to step out into the cold, knowing full well this isn't his final destination, just to see mothers reprimanding children with heavy-lidded eyes and tiny down jackets. There are no fathers here on the Metro-North. The woman from Pawling stands next to him, shivering, and pulls her scarf up to cover her mouth. 'Boyfriend loves this weather,' she says. 'I can't understand it.'

'No kidding.' Louis doesn't usually let himself think about the girl and the Housatonic River like that, unless – as is the case now – he feels like being cruel to himself. The full thought of her blooming through his head would be enough to send him into a panic, so he imagines her slowly. The small of her back, the hollow of her collarbone, the nape of her neck, all swelling out in his vision with a tenderness that's shocking.

'Here's the train,' the woman says. Louis knows intrinsically that avoiding her via a different carriage won't be an option any more. Together they have crossed some invisible threshold that makes ignoring her a type of disrespect falling somewhere outside the sphere of acceptable public transport rudeness. Louis turns his attention to the woods and spots a bunch of attractive-looking sumac growing just beyond the platform. Bright red masses, crested with white, popping up like hopeful little flames throughout the snow. He glances down and notices the woman's legs are bare underneath her long boots. Craziness, no wonder she's cold. Before she can catch him looking Louis turns his gaze back to the trees, her blue kneecaps adding to the list of body parts in his mind. He feels ashamed of himself, as he does almost constantly, and hopes that the woman can't see the marks of winter upon him as easily as he sees them upon her.

***

They make it quite a long way, to Scarsdale almost, before she starts talking again. Louis feigned an unconvincing sleep from Chappaqua to Valhalla, hoping the woman realised that was nothing more than a display of his own unique brand of politeness. Out of her handbag she grabs a small compact mirror, and starts rubbing a beige powder in circular motions across her cheeks. She notices Louis watching her.

'Bit difficult to do this on the train,' the woman says.

'To me, that just looks difficult full stop.' Louis doesn't think she really needs to wear the powder at all, and goes to tell her so, but restrains himself before he can entertain the notion aloud. Too weird, to tell a stranger they have nice skin.

'What,' she says, 'you've never worn makeup before?'

'No.' He thinks about it for a second. 'Should I have?'

'I don't know.' She laughs. 'I was under the impression that all men are closeted transvestites to some degree.'

Louis feels the sides of his face crinkling up into what he thinks might resemble a smile. If they weren't on a train right now, both suspended in this unusual vessel of non-reality – if they were on a beach or in a bar or even a dirty alleyway somewhere, anywhere – he would ask her out for a coffee. Louis is all at once struck by a sudden and acute awareness of the way he's dressed. These good-for-nothing studio clothes make his body look as cheap and flimsy as a puppet's. He glances down and observes the flesh of his knee poking through a worn section of pants. Louis has never given much thought to his knees before; all they represent to him is one component of a more substantial whole. Louis can remember a time when he was proud of his body and the way it functioned. Now his biceps and chest and rhomboids and pectorals may as well be made from the same thing as the stuffing in a cushion – sticking out in all the appropriate places without necessarily offering anything to anyone.

The woman flips her mirror shut, grabbing her handbag from the floor of the train and placing it on her lap. She drops the compact back into the depths of it and rummages around in there for a while, finally dragging out a battered iPhone. She offers it to Louis, nodding, and he takes it, a picture of her and someone who he assumes is her boyfriend stare back cheerfully at him from the screen. Despite him being clothed in full fireman's gear, the couple couldn't look any more suburban if they tried. Standing in front of a well-manicured house, a scattering of leaves adorning their front yard like individual treasures from Mother Nature herself. The whole thing is so perfect-looking Louis's surprised there's not a giant red ribbon across the scene just waiting to be snipped in the manner of an immaculately wrapped gift.

'It's going to be nice to have him home,' the woman says.

***

The concept of home has always been one of Louis's more distracting preoccupations in that he never quite knows how to think about it. Sometimes he feels like he doesn't need one; usually this happens at the turning of a season, when the whole earth is charged with a restless energy that can make anywhere feel fresh and new again. Sometimes, when he's sitting on his front porch in the afternoon sunshine, and the woods across from his house are wonderfully backlit, he notices the silhouettes of chipmunks and squirrels and crickets of all kinds moving about their business in such an easy-going way, and wonders if maybe he's home already. There was even a phase in his life when Louis thought New York City might have made an appropriate residence. But that was when he was still under the impression there was something else waiting for him there other than infinite anonymity. All Louis knows is that whenever he and the girl made love, it felt like stepping through the front door of his house after a long and exhausting vacation. How unfortunate that, out of them all, this was the home he chose.

***

Harlem is the last stop before Grand Central Station, and Louis always marvels at just how closely the people here live to the train line. Louis's carriage is passing right next to bedroom windows, just above or below the hundreds of homes situated in those tense, brown apartment buildings, and he feels like, if he leaned out just slightly, he would almost be able to snatch the laundry hanging from a sixth story balcony. Louis is aware of the woman performing the same sort of scrutiny as he is, so he murmurs, 'How can people live like this?'

She turns to him. 'What do you mean?'

'Well,' he says. Louis must not have understood that they were looking at the same view but thinking different things. 'You know, just all packed in like that.'

'You think they're unhappy.'

'I don't know. I would be.'

'Some of them probably are,' she says. 'But that's statistically inevitable.'

'So right now, in these buildings, people are dying and going broke and falling out of love with each other, while we're on the Metro.' Was this too morbid for train-talk? Louis couldn't tell.

'Of course they are. That's just life, though, isn't it?' She smiles at him but Louis looks away, back out the window, at the never-ending spectacle of brown bricks.

'You know that Harlem was where Ellington found his fame?' The woman's obviously worried she's upset him now.

'Is he what you would call a statistical anomaly?'

'No. That was just a random example of a man living his life. He probably rode the Metro-North a few times too.'

Grand Central Station, folks. This is the end of the line. Grand Central Station! Louis feels a sensation in his belly correlating directly with the realisation that his day has officially started. He knows that in just a moment he's going to emerge out of the underground, pass by the food court, and disappear into a crowd of people who are all on their way to somewhere better than this. The woman stretches her arms above her head and Louis lets her stand first, following her to the doors, positioning his body behind her as though she's the last thing between him and New York City.

'I hope you have a nice day with your boyfriend,' Louis says. She turns to look at him and he notices her face properly for the first time. Plain, really. Unremarkable. He tries to think of a way to describe her but all he can come up with is *green-eyed*.

'Thanks. Have a good day at work.' And that's it. No song and dance, no fuss, no tragedy or blessing or love story or even anything important – though it is easy for Louis to wish that their meeting had been something important. The woman adjusts her coat again as the train doors open, and Louis stirs, caught in the flood of bodies moving towards the light.

There is a wind down Fifth Avenue that seems to be blowing Louis in the right direction. Rockefeller Center stands stoically there in front of him, as ice-skaters skip and frisk like ants around its base. Louis wonders if it would be unethical to quit his job right here and now. Forget the two weeks' notice and instead run screaming *I'm outta here, motherfuckers!* to Upstate New York and sleep in a poor farmer's barn for the rest of his life. Waking up slowly on a hay bale somewhere in the company of fragrant pines – that might just make this life bearable.

Louis stops, unsure of where he's going, and stares a challenge up at the sky, waiting until the sun turns his retinas to jelly. Maybe the farmer who owns the barn will have a nice, strawberry-blonde daughter, and maybe that's how he'll spend the rest of his time – liaising with willowy farm girls from Connecticut all the way to Maine. Living off stolen apples and wild, buttery lettuce.

Louis looks down and realises there's a large black blob taking up most of his vision, so he sits beneath a nearby linden and waits for it to dissipate. The Fifth Avenue wind blows strongly and Louis is surprised to find a shower of heart-shaped leaves descending on him from above. Despite everything, the linden has somehow managed to keep a great deal of its foliage. The blackness is mostly gone now so he stares up at the sun again, but not directly, not as a challenge this time. Only as a casual observer, a tourist, looking upon it with a reverence usually reserved for great monuments or women's bodies. The giant orb, old and undemanding, still tracking the same unhurried course across a big, affectionate sky. It's like he's only realising now that it's been here this whole time.

Ironing

Jenny Macaulay

She stood as she ironed, with a gentle smile
Relaxed, not felt in a long, long while
And the rain beat down on the earth outside
Watering the feijoa.
In dreamy thought over hours and hours
Pressing tea towels, sheets and a silky blouse
She gracefully let the iron slide
Slowly, calmly, slower.
But she glanced at the bruise on her upper arm
Where, a hundred times, he had meant no harm
The purple now just a yellow hue
And the painful throb subsiding
With head held high she stretched her spine
And verbalised, 'The wardrobe's mine,
You bastard, you have got your due,'
And the iron kept on sliding.
And the rain beat down on the earth outside
As the iron thrust on a wilder ride
Over garments, torn with bloody stains
Then folded, oh so neatly.
She'd feared those nights in his white starched shirts
And drunken force up under skirts
But ironing soothed those tears and pains
Resolving, oh so sweetly.
Gone fishing, they thought with anguished dread
Been rough just off Indented Head
She packed the iron and board away
And gazed upon the garden.
She made herself a cup of tea,
It felt quite strange to feel so free
Like the breeze that made that fruit tree sway
And a heart she'd learnt to harden.
Weeks on, coming home in a howling gale
With her groceries, wine and the daily mail
She saw a card as she dropped her coat

On which her name sat boldly.
The back was blank so she tore the seal
To see what inside might reveal
And withdrew a handwritten torn-edged note
Which made her blood run coldly.
'Don't think I don't know what you've done
You'll pay me and my newborn son
Unless you'd like a prison cage
For I will blow your cover.'
A smudge of sliced feijoa flesh
Its perfume strong though not so fresh
Was smeared across the crumpled page
Just signed, 'Your husband's lover.'

Death wish
Johanna Stapleton

She hung teapots from the tree in her front yard as a warning, like heads on spikes, to make them all think twice. It was becoming quite a collection. Almost thirty of them hung from meticulously chosen branches, strung by their handles. In the warmer months, they were mere dots of pearly porcelain twinkling between the leaves. In winter, the tree did not complain through its annual shame of being stripped bare. It was stark against the sodden skies, except for its galaxy of rainbow baubles.

***

The collection started with just one.

Hurled at the door as he left, on the morning of her twenty-third birthday. Aiming for his face. His smug face. A smug mug, irritating like a bug she couldn't manage to swat. She wanted to wipe that smile away, maybe take away some of his undeserved beauty. Somehow, the fact of his handsomeness made it so much worse. More humiliating. She should have known that there would be a price for being the centre of his world for those short years.

It had never been a logical pairing, the artist and the butcher. His attention burned with a fierce intensity, like sun through a magnifying glass. It scared her. She was his Josephine, his Juliet, his Cleopatra. It was only logical that such a bright flame would die sooner than most.

She often lay awake in the early hours of the morning, staring blankly at the dim light that gradually crept across the ceiling. Imagining a terrible accident. Frozen to death in the meat storage freezer at his shop. Or maybe he would be run over by a garbage truck, his beautiful face mashed into the gravel. Only a few weeks before, she had seen photographs in the newspaper of a woman whose face was ripped off by a chimpanzee. The thickened skin had hung from her bones like lumps of wax, with crudely carved holes for her eyes, her mouth and the place where her nose used to be. In a strange irony, her expression was fixed in a look of absolute tranquillity.

A roughly carved Madonna.

On that morning, in the hours after he left, she crawled along the skirting board, collecting the pieces of porcelain. They were all there. She spread glue along the porous edges and pressed them together with bloodless fingers until all hints of violence were gone. But the glue could only do so much. Tea dribbled out from invisible fissures. It held together, structurally sound, but it could never serve its purpose again. A teapot allergic to tea. It was too pretty to throw away, so she kept it on the mantelpiece.

It was a month before he came home, dragging a duffel bag of dirty clothes and a deflated ego.

'Things with Stephanie didn't work out,' he said, shrugging his shoulders. 'Anyway, maybe this was good for us. It's just a little hiccup. I needed that time to realise how much I love you.'

She was unmoved, staring at the bag and mentally unpacking it. Would there be lipstick on his collars, or was that too much of a cliché? It was so pedestrian. Affairs never looked like this in the movies. She was meant to scream and cry, and throw him out into the street. It was meant to be the end of the world. She wanted to be angry, but instead she shut down. It was too much effort to fight. A yearning for normality took over as her cold fury melted away, all her disappointment condensed to a stony lump in her core. Her fingers ached to pick through her husband's cotton shirts and hold them to her face, inhaling that signature mix of sweat and cologne. She wanted nothing more than to wash his clothes, fix him dinner and lie beside his warm body. Everything could be just as it was before.

A little while later, he bought her a new teapot, even prettier than the last. Dainty and duck egg blue, with Chinese peach blossoms decorating the handle. It was so different from anything he would have chosen before. She wondered what had possessed him to buy such a beautiful thing for his dowdy little mouse of a housewife. What kind of woman could inspire such a beautiful thought? She turned the painted porcelain over in her hands as though it belonged to someone else.

A vision rushed into her consciousness, like a waking dream where she could watch herself from outside her body. She watched as her cautious smile turned to a grimace and she smashed the teapot into his temple rather than into the wall. He groaned and pitched forward, blood dripping from the wound.

She blinked, relieved as reality came back into focus. She looked at the teapot and smiled, considering it an olive branch, and forgave every last thing.

***

She had never been a collector of anything, not on purpose. The teapots just seemed to multiply by themselves. Every relic had a name. There was a Rosie, a Helena, an Isobel. There was an Anna, then an Anna II (after the second time). She didn't know why it was so important to her to keep them but she couldn't bear to throw them away. Despite their faults.

Her husband, when he was home, was a dream.

He planted roses by the French windows, so she could paint them in every season. She painted them again and again, marvelling at how much they could change in the space of a single day. Tight buds would slowly swell and erupt into full blooms, only to be dashed by a rainstorm. With the petals decimated by the weather, she found them even more interesting. The soft organic shapes that wrapped around each other to form each bloom seemed almost lonely by themselves.

On summer nights, he would sit on the back step in the moonlight, sharpening his butcher's knives with a special stone, humming a tune from a song that he only half-remembered. When his work was done, he would come inside and sleep in the safe cocoon of lovingly ironed sheets.

She lay next to him, listening to the gentle rhythm of his breathing long into the night. After the first time he left, she never slept soundly again. Sleep was something to be snatched in tiny handfuls, here and there, or whenever she could no longer resist it. She took long naps during the day while he was at work but couldn't bring herself to sleep while he was around.

When she was a little girl, she had never been allowed to go on sleepovers at her friends' houses in case *it* happened. There was always a risk that she would go to bed and wake up streets from home or in the next-door neighbour's swimming pool. She would wake up with gravel-scuffed feet, grass in her hair and no memory of her night activities. Entire tubs of ice cream would disappear from the freezer and she would wake up with sticky fingers and a stomach-ache. Once, after a particularly nasty fight with her mother, she had filled every single page of her diary with the same three words: *I hate her.*

Sleep was a gateway for all her inhibitions. Whatever lurked inside her, whether she knew it or not, would find a way to come out when she slept. A part of her wanted so badly to hurt her husband, to make him suffer, so she couldn't take that risk. The most important thing was to stay alert. She gazed at his sleeping form, the rise and fall of his chest, the flutter of his eyelashes against his cheek.

He never even knew her secret.

***

'What time will you be home?'

She held the phone a little too tightly, waiting for his response.

'When I'm home.'

She could always feel it coming. Clues crept into every interaction. A little extra rush to leave the house in the morning. A distracted look. Something forgotten or overlooked. A gaze held for a fraction of a second less.

On the weekend, he gave the roses their winter prune. He hacked the bushes down to sticks, stark like skewers sticking out of the ground. Afterwards he went out. 'With the boys,' he said. She knew better. She paced the empty house with a growing impatience, wishing that he could get this latest dalliance out of his system and skip straight to the inevitable homecoming.

It frightened her, how easily she had slipped into the long-suffering wife routine, but she couldn't see any other way through it. So much hurt and betrayal for little moments of wonderful. But even through the good times there was a thorny undercurrent.

It was constant, like low-frequency static that hummed almost undetectably through every conscious moment.

She hated him almost as fiercely as she loved him. She wished him dead, shot through the heart with poison-tipped arrows and torn apart by wild animals. But she also wanted nothing more than for him to come home, take her in his arms and kiss her like she was the most precious woman on Earth.

***

'I'm not coming back this time,' he said.

She kept her gaze fixed, studying a small crack that rose up the wall from the skirting board, willing herself to disappear. Maybe, if she wished hard enough, she could turn every atom in her body into a vapour. She would rise up the chimney and dissipate, misting all the microscopic particles of her entire being over the suburbs. Like dust, like rain.

'It's for the best, love.' He grabbed his bag and practically skipped out the front door.

She blinked, realising with disappointment that she was still whole. The scene played out like a dream, and she was only a mute observer. A thick, translucent mass of fog clung to the ground, like they were standing knee-deep in milk. The street was utterly deserted. Except for the roar of the approaching garbage truck, there was not a single sign of life.

He swung his bag as he walked, giddy with anticipation. Meaning to cross the road after the truck had passed, he walked too close. The dangling strap of his duffel bag swung out and became tangled in some infernal piece of hardware on the side of the truck. Before he had the presence of mind to let go, the driver accelerated, yanking him off his feet and sending him stumbling under the wheel.

No scream.

The truck rolled over the little bump and drove on, unaware.

'Oh no.' She sprinted out into the street in her nightgown, her breath scraping her throat like a knife. Her jelly legs stumbled through the fog to the place where he had fallen, searching for him.

His ankles, knees and hips bent at extreme angles, like a crumpled puppet. A grimy tyre print marked the shoulder of his white shirt, leading towards his head.

She didn't need to check his pulse. Nobody could survive that.

With considerable effort, she peeled him off the road and cradled his body in her arms. His face was a mess. Like a squashed melon. Blood trickled from his mouth and nose, travelling along the burst seams of his skin. The dimensions of his jaw and cheekbones were all wrong.

Only his skin kept the shattered bones together.

Nobody had seen it happen. All the practicalities of the situation eluded her.

Wasn't she meant to cry or call the police? She dragged the body up the garden path and into the house, his cracked skull hitting the doorstep with a pulpy thud. His body lay sprawled on the kitchen floor. She felt the creeping terror that all those tiny moments, where she hated him and wished him dead, had added up to something inescapable.

'Shh,' she whispered into his bloody ear, rocking him. 'You're home now. And you'll never leave again.'

***

She painted the roses for the hundredth time, working the paint in a new layer over an old canvas. Rewriting the old, retelling the same story.

All she had left of him was a bag of bones, boiled clean like something from a high-school science room. Her fingers ran over their chalky topography, remembering the way they used to feel when they were clothed in flesh. The cheekbone that pressed tight against the shallow cave of her eye socket each time they kissed. The tiny remnants of fingertips that once combed through her hair.

She never could bring herself to call an ambulance. There was never any hope, and it was just too much to think of him being taken away from her again. She kept his body, not knowing what to do with it other than to stash it in the cellar. All sorts of infernal insects rose up from the dirt floor to claim their share of his flesh. In a year, he was nothing but bones and hair. She took his wedding ring then calmly gathered the pieces of his skeleton.

With only the bone saw from his butchery tools, the work was slow. She managed a little every day. White dust coated her hands like talcum powder. When she was done, she gathered the fragments and walked through the empty house to the garden where once she had dragged his lifeless body. She reached up into the branches of the tree and bent the branches towards her, distributing the pieces of her husband's bones into those innocuous hanging teapots, replacing the little lids, leaving their secrets tucked safely inside.

She could finally sleep. The bitter core was gone. Everything was in its right place.

Wino

Krystle Herdy

i had thought by now that I would be able to differentiate
between good and bad wine.
had thought by now, that
i would no longer have to tally up copper-nickel plated coins
just to afford holes in my wasted lungs.
a stranger passing by yells,
why don't you just light a twenty dollar bill on fire
and suck back on that?
i tell her,
the same reason you ornament yourself in
cork-wedged heels and sixty dollar Siddhartha Gautama t-shirts;
because sometimes it can be hard, this breathing just for one.
tonight,
she will fix her legs into a crucifix for the first man
who says he would die for her sins
and i will walk the fluorescent aisles of an after-hours bottle shop,
still unenlightened by the disparity
between a good drop and a bad.

Violets in a spring thunderstorm

Tamsin Martin

Crumpled madams of pleasure
Fold weakly over the cool
Bars of the iron gate
Clinging, as drops pool
On their bright purple petals
In a gleaming school.
A bold one, head back
Exposes her pure core
She wears the stain of rain
Proudly, the whore!
And loved the tormenting storm
Opening her like a sore
A growl of thunder warns, then
Bright flash and sharp crack
The sudden downpour
Pounds flower-flesh, thwack!
Thwack! Needles of rain
In armies that sting and smack
Wild bunch of bobbing, sodden
Heads in untidy rows
You have a fragrance to madden
Fresh and sweet, it sows
A hotbed of longing
Blooming under my nose.

Bad mum
Liam Donnelly

After you were born I would lie there as people fussed over you, the white sheets pulled so tightly around me that all I could move was my head, but by that point I hardly had the motivation to move my head anyway. I had the little television that was hanging in the corner of the room turned on so people might think I was watching it and not talk to me. There was a constant stream of people coming in and out, but I would simply listen to the nurses nag and visitors spout clichés: *Wasn't I happy? Wasn't I just over the moon?* All Nanna could think to say was, 'Isn't he chubby?'

My stitches hurt and I looked like shit, and I nearly died when your dad shoved a camera in my face. I put on an expression of good humoured irritation and said, 'I'm not presentable,' though I knew then that I would never be presentable again. But that was the least of my concerns. My life was over.

I hated being in the hospital and yet I never wanted to go home. How could I bring a baby back to my shithole of a house? I mean, we had planned for it to be more … welcoming, by the time you arrived.

It was a house that the realtor had described as 'suitable for a growing family' and a 'renovator's dream'. I hated it. It was always cold. The floorboards gave me splinters. The wooden slats showed through missing patches of dry wall. You wouldn't have noticed, but your Nanna's judgements were like claws in my back. Yes, obviously I wasn't planning on leaving the couch there. *Does this room look finished to you? I just haven't figured out where to fit all my shit yet, all right?* And I had to find room for a baby as well.

I can almost laugh at how absolutely bonkers I was. But even twenty-two years later my face hurts when I think about the day we brought you home and I felt so weak that I dropped you on the floor. Your fall was partially broken by the thick blanket you were wrapped in, so all you got was a scratch on the head. I never told your dad, and he never said anything about the scratch. After that, I had recurring dreams in which I kept stepping on your head. I would wake from them and lie in bed next to your dad for the remainder of the night and listen to my head tell me how wrong I was, how *bad* I was.

I thought that if I just continued to lie there I would eventually be left alone. Your dad would stop filming, Nanna would fuck off and you would go to sleep, and I could have some quiet. But the quiet never came. I waited and I waited and I put on the right faces when I could be bothered and I laughed politely when I felt it was absolutely necessary and I let you literally suck the life out of me, but not once was I rewarded my few moments of silence.

If you look back on the home videos that your dad filmed during these months, you can hear Auntie Barb in the background ask me how I'm doing. I reply with, 'As good as can be expected.' She would have known I was lying. You are, of course, the focus of the film. Your cousins are each trying to get your attention. I'm probably just off-screen rolling my eyes. Another video was filmed at a fairy-themed birthday party for the daughter of my friend, Sheree. I'm sitting alone in the corner and this time when the camera is pointed on me I immediately cover my face with my hands. If you turn the volume up you'll hear me growl, 'Get fucked.'

Everyone around us knew I was on the verge of something – what that something was no one could be quite sure, but a feeling of dread was descending over the house. It made the air heavy. You could feel it just by stepping through the front door. Nanna knew, and so she would come over to my unsuitable-for-a-child house and care for you. She would bustle around, washing blankets and rinsing bottles. Whenever you cried I'd go and sit in the backyard and wait. Occasionally she would bring you outside and ask if I wanted to hold you, or feed you. I would say, 'Not right now, thanks,' and she would sigh and mutter something as she took you back in. Sometimes she would say things to me like, 'I just don't understand what your problem is,' and I wouldn't even bother to reply.

Nanna never approved of me, I knew that from the very beginning. When we first met she smiled graciously but her jaw was clenched. Maybe it was because I was older than your dad, maybe it was because I had already been divorced. It doesn't matter now.

I didn't have the energy to focus on a book, so I couldn't read. I wasn't able to listen to music. The piano, which I usually loved to play, was still covered with an old sheet from when we moved in. I didn't even have the energy to change my clothes. My hair was a matted mess. Once your dad told me I smelt and I wanted to claw both of our faces off.

I tried to hang myself using the cord of my tracksuit pants. I didn't bother to leave a note. I know how stupid that sounds, but I tied a loop around my neck and tied the other end around the ceiling fan while standing on the clothes basket that I had dragged from the laundry. I had to stand in it and stamp repeatedly on the overflowing clothes that had accumulated just so I could place the lid on it. I don't even know what that cord was made of, cotton? Nylon? Whatever it was, it snapped within two seconds. Landing on my hands and knees hurt like hell. It's such a strange feeling, thinking that everything is going to finish and then suddenly you're on the floor and the pain is shocking and your husband is running in and you're asking yourself, 'Why the fuck am I so stupid?' Either way, I couldn't pretend that everything was normal anymore.

After that first 'incident' – as Nanna labelled it – I was taken to hospital, but it was a different kind of hospital this time. At least by that stage people knew I wasn't fit to care for you and I didn't care that my big, dark secret was out.

Your dad thought some rest would improve my mental state, and I kind of thought it would too, but I continued to sink further and further. I can remember having to be bathed by Sheree. She was the single person who didn't make me feel like I was being a selfish bitch. She tried her hardest to care for me, but with a young child of her own she struggled to find the time and we only saw each other occasionally. I'm not sure where you were during those weeks I was in hospital. With Nanna I presume. I can't imagine you were left with your dad because he was hopeless. I don't mean to sound harsh – he had the best intentions, I know, but he found himself in a position that he was just not ready for.

Laying in my hospital bed I would listen to the various cries and moans of the other patients and contemplate my options. I would stare longingly at the thick cord connecting the television to the wall, but after my botched hanging attempt I didn't have the confidence to try that way again. The best option was to crash my car into a tree or a pole; the extra benefit of this being that you need never even know I went mad. You could live your life believing that your doting mother was tragically killed in a car accident during your infancy, and eventually everyone else would forget I even existed.

I enjoyed having the idea festering in my mind. I imagined what my car would look like after the crash. It was already a piece of junk that, conveniently for me, didn't have an airbag. I imagined what my body would look like inside it. The grisly images gave me a certain thrill. I was going to mangle my body to the point where my brain would have no other option than to stop. I also picked out the tree: a big old elm just around the corner from Nanna's house.

Once I had my plan sorted in my mind I felt light. The next morning I even put on makeup. All the nurses commented on how much brighter I looked. Nanna couldn't believe it. Upon seeing me she said, 'Well, isn't this a turn up for the books?' Then I washed my hair. Within a week I was sent home. I was cured!

I arrived home to discover that your dad had done all the things around the house that I had failed to do myself. There was a lamp by the bed. Books had been arranged on the shelves. He had even put a framed photo of us on top of the fridge. I opened the door and the only food inside was a bottle of tomato sauce.

That night I drove to my tree. It loomed ahead as I turned into the street. The tree swayed and rustled in the dry wind. A dull orange glow radiated from the streetlights. It shone through the branches, creating patches of light that slid across the road. I paused to take several deep breaths. A cat ran across the street and over a fence. *It's probably going to eat my face after I'm dead*, I thought. I remember wondering why it wasn't inside. I remember wondering why I wasn't inside. I was shocked at my own hesitance. I began to doubt my plan. I had chosen a stupid spot. I didn't have enough space to gain speed. Why did I choose a residential area? I turned off the engine and sat there, my knees shaking. Stupid, stupid, stupid.

I knew then that I had missed my chance. Once you lose your momentum it's hard to get it back. I started the car once again and drove towards my tree and then I drove past it. I drove away from Nanna and from my husband and from you. I drove until the sun peeked over the rooftops and into my eyes. I drove with the windows down, the breeze whipping my hair around my face. I ignored the phone calls that continued throughout that day and into the next. I imagined Nanna saying, hands on hips, 'What's she gone and done now?'

It's not like I really disappeared. I could have easily been found if anyone bothered to come looking for me. But Nanna never came looking for me. Your dad didn't either.

I remember the last conversation I had with your father quite vividly. It was on the day that I vanished. He said, 'I bet you're glad to be home. I am. Glad, I mean. Hopefully now things will be normal again.' He squeezed my hand, and I forced a smile.

I think about you sometimes, but it's easier not to. I wonder what you look like, what you sound like. I wonder if you know what I looked like. I'm not sure we'd even like each other if we met. I doubt you'd like me. I occasionally regret not seeing you grow up – even to see a picture would be nice – but I never regret leaving.

Remember, it wasn't your fault. But it wasn't mine either.

Sincerely,

Your bad mum.

Train approaching
Paul South

The tracks' instincts
are to coil and snake
but they are fastened by physics
and steel pins.
Still I feel them
squirming
like charmed ropes.

Ships of the desert
Carmel Lillis

1

'Toss you for it.' Orange spikes graze black curls, the chafe of dripping board-shorts forgotten as two boys lean in to inspect their find, abandoning their crab search for the ancient lure of the quintessential.

It was Omar who'd spotted the disc and chain half-buried in the sand when the scorching sun drove them to shelter beneath the arches of the pier. But it was his friend, Jack, who'd swooped on it before Omar's mouth had even formed the words *Finders Keepers*; it was Jack who'd scoured the surface with a coin to reveal the weird writing; and it is Jack who holds it aloft now, proposing possession be decided on a coin flip.

Omar, feeling his pulse quicken, knows he must submit – that to explain why it is so essential that he have the disc would be to risk ridicule he just isn't up for.

Jack dangles the disc by its chain, while Omar tosses a dollar coin into the sunlight and calls *heads* before it lands. Tails faces up.

'Best of three?' says Omar. Another throw – they call it even. On some unspoken certainty that a verdict delivered on solid ground will be fairer than a decision rising from sand drifting with each return of tide, they shift to the footpath. The whirling coin hits the concrete. It rolls. Spins. Slower, slower. Finally it gives up and lays still, heads down, tails up.

Omar's breathing shallows.

Jack says, 'Now don't go all butt-hurt on me.'

Omar's fists clench, but he shrugs. 'Prob'ly rubbish anyway.'

With the edge of the coin, and then with his fingernail, Jack scrapes sand grains from the clasp, prises it open, and pulls the chain out of the pierced hole. 'I bet it's gold,' he smiles, as he pockets the chain and flings the disc onto the wet sand.

Omar's mouth falls open. He starts to speak.

Stops.

Stares.

'Oh hell, no,' Jack yells. As he leaps across the sand to retrieve their buckets bobbing the water, Omar scoops up the disc and cradles it in his palm. His breathing steadies.

Swinging their buckets, lamenting the holidays ended too soon, chattering about the moves to different schools, probing rumours of standover dudes from senior classes and dismissing them as bullshit, the friends traipse the footpath fringing the sand.

At the corner, they shuffle about and recount their crabs. They gaze at the bay as if for the last time. For a rare minute, they cannot speak. Silver-tipped waves rippling like giant bird wings; sand so pure it looks vacuumed. Even the seafood processing works, stripped back to its framework, marooned like a giant fish skeleton – if he could capture this in paint, Omar would call it 'Perfection'. If only it didn't remind him of his mum losing her job. Of the spin-offs: dropped high school enrolments, redundancies, his dad having to go away …

'Arab writing, look. Like on that medal thingy.' Jack is pointing to a container ship way out, crossing the horizon. 'Reckon a sailor from the Sahara dropped it overboard?'

'Sure,' says Omar, snapped back into the moment. 'Like ships always hang out in deserts?'

They laugh and push each other, the ache for their childhoods' passing absorbed in their wrestle.

2

Adam Smith is packing his case. At least, he's been hunching on the double bed beside his case for an hour, his angular frame dwarfed by the half-dozen pillows Mary has plumped.

Mary bustles in, ironed shirts over her arm. Sighs.

'Sit with me,' he pleads.

Mary tut-tuts over underwear tossed in a heap.

Adam puts his hand on her arm. 'Mary, Mary,' he whispers. 'The suffering up there, you wouldn't believe.'

'First day back, always hard. Exactly what I told Omar. Just push through, Adam.'

He sprawls across the bed, sending the case clattering, scattering the ironing and gulping into a pillow, 'I can't.'

Mary's voice is sharpened flint. 'You're not a child. You must. What will become of us if you don't?'

'What will become of me if I do? What will become of us then?' he sobs.

One by one, she retrieves items from the floor, shop-folding, flattening into piles. 'Only six weeks, Adam. Then – three weeks together.'

'Six weeks,' he cries. 'In a detention centre, six weeks makes an imminent death sentence desirable.'

Mary's voice breaks as she says, 'Any job is better than no job.'

He reaches for her again, but she draws back. Sorting, tucking in corners on perfect piles of t-shirts, she stops only when a shadow falls across the doorway.

'Omar, back from the beach. Sit up, Adam.'

When Adam straightens, and stretches his mouth into a smile, Mary retreats to cook their last dinner.

3

'You heard? You saw?' Adam Smith is begging.

Omar Smith is grasping, for any lie at all. 'I saw ... your case. I was looking at my crabs mostly, but.'

The man reaches for his boy as if for a toddler. Omar stands unbending, listening to the thump of his own heart, his face scorched. At last he says, 'Can you translate this, Dad?' He holds out the disc that has sweated, and cut, into his palm.

And they are both glad of it. The father sends his boy for polish. Omar wastes time shuffling bottles in the cleaning cupboard, and returns to find his father checking his toiletries bag.

In turns they scrub, until the cloth blackens and the disc gleams. 'Look Omar, how the letters travel from right to left. *In this grey desert, a flamboyant flame are you.*' Adam turns the medal over. 'Now, engraved here, a tiny ship, prow pointed right. What do these strokes and loops tell us? Ah, yes. *May you never become a nameless droplet in a nameless sea.* Finishes with the ornamental flourish characteristic of Arabic.'

Omar loves his father like this – a teacher, a wise man. Not a boy-man like himself. Not a father even more boy than himself.

For Omar had not sobbed at the prospect of leaving Jack to travel by bus away from his bay, to a school where rumour has it that bullies stalk and pounce any time. Well, he really had cried, but not where anyone could see.

'What d'you reckon, Dad? Maybe it belonged to a sailor. Maybe he leant over too far, or ... maybe his girlfriend ditched him and he tossed it away.'

'Or a refugee, this medal the only thing a shark didn't swallow.' His father looks as if he might cry again.

Say something, anything. 'Weird combination, yeah? Ships and deserts.'

'Ships of the desert?'

'Dumb, yeah?'

'Dumb? No. That's what they called the first Afghanis in Australia. The people my mother descended from. Cameleers in the outback – ships of the desert.'

Whenever Omar had heard bits of this story, his eyes had glazed and later, he could remember little of it. But now he listens intently, prompting when his father pauses. Anything to keep his father from crying about refugees.

Perhaps it's the finding of the disc, perhaps it's because he'll be twelve soon, but this time he can picture the horses of more than a hundred years ago writhing in parched agony in the red desert. He can see the camel trains, led by the Afghanis – tall and proud, transporting supplies to settlements in the dusty outback. He can hear the squeals of skinny children with sunburnt skin peeling from their faces, rushing to greet them as they bring water and equipment and bags of chaff. 'The backbone of Australia, the Afghan cameleers. Ships of the desert,' his father declares again.

And then Adam tells of how, when the cameleers were no longer needed, most had felt rejected, and had left. A few, old and abandoned, sheltered in the first mosque. But his own ancestor was the exception – he raised a family, passing on the language, the sayings, even the name choices.

Yeah, those embarrassing sayings. *Let's stop to water the camels,* his father had said when they'd taken Jack on a road trip and pulled in for petrol. But then Jack had recounted how his great-grandfather, when they took him in the car, kept saying weird things like *Give her her head,* and when he thought they were going too fast, he'd yelled *Rein her in,* as if his mum was steering a horse. So they'd finished up laughing about the weirdness of adults, and Omar had felt better.

'Life's not so easy sometimes, is it? Wasn't back then. Still isn't.' His father plunges into the thick of Omar's thoughts.

'You said there wasn't any five minutes we couldn't live through.' Omar wonders who is comforting whom. 'You take the medal, Dad. Good luck charm. I brought it back for you. 'Cos you're going away.'

When his father hugs him, Omar doesn't stiffen as he might have just yesterday.

'You'll do fine tomorrow, Mate. Day one soon done.'

'You too, Dad. Five minutes at a time, yeah?'

'They'll collect me off the plane, same time you're waking in the morning. I'll think of you, in your smart uniform, as you board the bus. My gate will clang behind me round the time you enter your school gate.' The father grips the talisman. 'I'll carry this in my pocket. You'll be there with me, and we'll both make it through.'

4

Omar hears his mother making little smacking sounds. He pictures her in front of the mirror applying her red lipstick, kissing one lip against the other. Silent as an intruder, he eases himself from bed and tiptoes to the door. With one hand Mary is feathering her lashes with a swizzle; in the other, she holds the lash curler.

She hears her son, or she senses him. Her face reddens deeper than her blush. 'Go back to bed. You've a big day tomorrow.'

'You going out?'

'Dad wants me to. Well, he would want me to. So don't you go making trouble.'

Omar quivers as if he's been struck. 'I ... Will you be back before school?'

'Oh, Omar. When haven't I been here to cut your lunch, and see you off?'

She puckers her lips, beckons him. He flinches and does not move. She says, 'All right. That's best. I don't want to smear lipstick on you.' He hears a car horn toot long and hard, and his mother's light voice: 'Back to bed. That's what Dad would want.' She blows him a kiss as she high-heels across the tiles.

Omar lies awake, remembering how for so long, he never understood anything, and wishing, wishing he could return to being the naive boy he was yesterday.

5

Omar dreams his father is shaking him like he's a bag of chaff, and wakes to find his father shaking him like he's a bag of chaff.

'What ... Dad ... why?'

In the electric glare, Omar blinks, every muscle craving sleep. The wrack of his father's sobs ripples through his own body. 'Dad? The plane. Shouldn't you be ...' He cannot focus; he cannot think. 'You forget something? Books? What?'

Steadying himself, Omar retrieves his phone from under his pillow. 1.18. 'Dad, did you miss your plane?'

'Your mother. I rang her. From the airport. Music. Bar. Party. Not home. Not home music.'

'A little while. Mum's just going a little ...'

'You knew? Omar? Traitor. My own son.'

'No, no. Tonight. Only tonight. She's going to make my lunch ... she said so, Dad.'

His father releases Omar's pyjama top and drops his head onto the boy's chest. 'I'm sorry. I'm sorry.'

For the second time in a few hours, and the second time in his life, Omar is seeing his father cry. He feels tears sting behind his own lids and bites his lip to stop it wobbling. Wide awake now, he begins to reason. 'Mum will have just gone to a movie with her girlfriends.' He pats his father's black curls, so like his own, legacy of the man who drove the ships of the desert.

His father's sobs quieter now, Omar says, 'Dad, I'll sit up with you. She'll be home soon. I know it.'

The silence between them stretches across the minutes, into the chiming of the hour of two. 'Dad,' says Omar, desperate to stop his father's pacing, 'tell me what you do with the refugees.'

At first, Adam's talk flits and darts. But as he warms to his topic, he tells his boy how he divides his time between adults who cling to learning English like a lifeline when the past holds only death; and the children. Kids with dull eyes, whose mothers bring them to the classroom, a respite from heat and red sand that blows into their mouths and even their ears. He talks of how writing is a kind of therapy for them.

'Want to read one of their stories?' Omar watches his father rifle through a wad of papers. 'Here,' Adam says. 'You'll get some idea.'

Can it be true? Mr Smith likes the zoo, where lions are kept in cages. He says where he comes from, they have a zoo with so much space and greenery, animals don't know they are in cages. He says when we get out, he will introduce me to his boy, Omar, and we will all go to the zoo in the city. I want to see the city, I want to meet Omar. But do I want to go to the zoo? I am not sure.

Can cages be all right if you don't know you are inside one? Trouble is, humans always know. Playing basketball in a gym, a nice gym, you cannot forget it is a gym inside a cage of electric wire. Lights in cages; caged cameras stalking you. When everything is in cages, all you think about is getting out, not scoring goals.

'Why don't you draw like you used to?' Mother encourages. She longs for pictures of flowers stretching to a glowing sun against dappled blue-black sea. But you draw what you see: you sketch your people, you draw barbed wire in front of them. Even in front of the babies who can't walk, let alone run away, you draw barbed wire. You draw the wild man, with hair and beard like a lion's mane, pacing all day behind the wire.

In the night, you wake with the cold sweat pouring off you. 'I just heard the electric gates clang. They're stuck.'

Mother reasons: 'We're too far back to hear.' You start to explain, but when you try to speak of things that matter, the desert winds carry your voice away.

Desert on four sides. Have the people who ordered the cages ever thought where the kids might escape to? Just one road out, through a desert. The desert is its own cage. Yet they put iron grilles over the windows; they bolt steel tables and chairs into a concrete base.

Inside the donga one night, Mother switches on the light to comfort a whimpering woman. The woman is still asleep, wailing in some far-off land she refuses to travel to when she's awake. In daylight, she is a smiley woman. She minds her children, she smiles; she washes clothes, she smiles. You cannot understand what she says, yet when she speaks to you, she speaks the same language as Mother. The language of love.

But at night she battles people you cannot see, in a language you never want to learn.

After that, Mother doesn't get up when people whimper and scream. Sometimes though, she reaches her hand down from the bunk above. Stretching, you touch her fingertips. And you dare to believe you will leave one day, and live in a place where there are no—

A key scrapes through the keyhole. Heels click over tiles. A mother calls, 'Omar, what are …' and then she stops, his lovely mother with the red gone from her lips, and her cheeks deepening to scarlet.

Omar puts his hands over his ears, and runs to his bedroom. He lies there a long time, thinking of the disc and feeling himself shrivel – a nameless droplet in a nameless sea.

6

Omar, in a blazer whose shoulders seam almost at his elbows, waits with his father. His mother hovers. When their taxi pulls up, Omar lets her kiss him, but he does not return it.

Adam, his eyes ringed in sooty black, hugs Mary for what seems to Omar the longest time. He says to the driver, 'Airport please,' but asks him to detour first to Omar's school, several kilometres inland.

'Poor Mum, her job gone. Now her boys,' Adam says as he fumbles for his seatbelt. In his father's face, Omar sees only love; no trace of last night's angst.

Last night, Omar remembered, he felt so small and so old. Today, with his hands disappearing up his too-long blazer sleeves, he is still small, but with his father smiling, he is young again. He swings around to smile at the tiny dressing-gowned figure in the driveway, her hand frozen in a half-wave.

They travel in silence until the glint of the bay morphs into the glint of glass towers. Adam taps the disc in his pocket. 'It'll remind us,' he whispers. 'We're ships of the desert, carriers of hope in hard places. So spend time with Mum sometimes when I'm away. Okay?'

'I'll try.' The day will be withering – Omar can already feel the sting. 'Dad, what your student wrote. How did it end?'

'It hasn't.'

'That's why you're going back, yeah? Miss you, but.'

'I'm going for them; for us, too.'

Omar asks if the taxi can stop a street away. Before he climbs out, his father shakes his hand.

Omar watches the taxi pull into traffic, then he hoists his bag high and crosses the road towards his new school.

Meridian post/ante

Ben Walter

<pre>
certain noon or midnight,
        the mail clock fixed,
                {what is the}
        a beginning,
                {what is the}
  though high hours
        (duels? witches?)
        weary posts transgressed;
                {what is the}
        analogue precision
                unblinking,
        a now (face) reputed,
                {what is the}
  each day orients my when
        nowhen; early or late,
                {what   is   the}
        meeting middle hours,
        high above.
</pre>

Paradise
Aaron Peysack

Malone woke in a small windowless room. He felt like a man who has returned from a long journey to find his house isn't where it used to be. The only piece of furniture was the chair he was sitting in, which looked familiar though he couldn't say where he'd seen it. On the far side of the room was a door. He knew he would have to open it eventually, but for now he felt no desire to move; he was content just to sit there following the flow of his own thoughts. If he waited long enough, someone would come, and if they didn't, they didn't.

It was some time before Malone realised he wasn't alone. Something very small had begun to move across the wall and, as Malone looked on, it assumed the shape and proportions of a common housefly. I must have brought it with me, he thought. The curious thing about the fly was that it made no attempt to escape Malone when he approached; on the contrary, it crawled onto his hand and remained there, watching him intently, the way a child watches a television screen in the late afternoon.

After several minutes, when it was clear to him that no one was coming, Malone walked across the room and put his ear to the door. What he heard was extraordinary. It was as though an insect were tunnelling through the wood and he could hear every sound it made, even the scraping of its teeth against the grit; and beyond the wood, the sea or something like the sea, trapped in a shell, a chamber without walls. It was both beautiful and frightening. He doesn't remember how long he stood there listening, a quarter of an hour, maybe more. His body felt light, almost weightless, like a cosmonaut dancing on the moon. A sense of peace came over him; he hadn't felt that way in such a long time.

Eventually he freed himself from the door and stepped into the passage, which was empty – no sea, no sound, just a long white wall, unadorned, like the halls of an old hospital that has been abandoned after a war. At the end of the corridor a man was sitting on a bench with his hands resting on his knees. The man was waiting for him, that much was clear, but who he was or why he was waiting Malone couldn't say. He remembered the first time he entered his father's study and saw the books along the walls and the maps laid out on the table and sensed the mystery of these things without being able to express it.

It took a long time for Malone to reach the end of the corridor. His legs felt heavy, as if someone had filled them with water. As he moved, the man watched him from his bench with the detached look of someone past caring. Malone was surprised he could see the eyes so clearly, not just the outline but the pupils themselves, dilated in the bright light of the corridor. They were a peculiar colour, neither brown nor green, but grey like the rooves of Paris.

The man got to his feet and walked a few steps towards Malone. 'Ready?' he said.

'I think so,' Malone said. 'How long was I asleep?'

The man shrugged. 'We don't keep records.'

'What if something happened?'

'Nothing happened.'

'But if it did?'

'What could happen?'

'I don't know, what if I didn't wake up?'

'They all wake up eventually; some take longer than others, that's all.'

'Did I take longer than most?'

'I have no idea. I only came up a few minutes ago. The other guy's sick so they called me.'

Malone stopped outside the elevators.

'They're broken,' the man said, 'we'll have to use the stairs. Don't touch the rails, they're unsteady.'

For some reason Malone thought he was only two or three floors up, but as they descended he realised they were actually much higher. The air was so thin he couldn't fill his lungs. He felt the same thing in Mexico, an awful panicky feeling like drowning in mid-air.

'Do you mind if we rest a minute?' he asked after a while. 'I'm a little short of breath.'

'Sure.'

The two of them sat down on the landing and Malone watched the man calmly remove a cigarette from one of his pockets and begin to smoke. After he exhaled he waved the smoke away.

'Is it much further?' Malone asked.

'If I say it is, what are you going to do, go back?'

'I was just wondering.'

'We'll get there when we get there,' the man said.

Malone nodded because there was nothing else to do. He would have liked to talk but the man's face and manner discouraged conversation. He gave the impression of someone wholly self-contained, impenetrable as a monkey sitting on the edge of the forest. He was wrong about the man's eyes, though: they were not grey like Paris rooves but an ordinary blue.

As far as Malone could tell there was no ventilation in the stairwell; the smoke from the man's cigarette hung in the air, forming a mist that others would have to walk through. He would have asked him to stop but he was afraid of the response. He could imagine the man saying something dismissive, even stubbing the cigarette out on Malone's hand. It occurred to him that he was being unfair, that the man had given no indication that he was capable of such behaviour. Malone had always been prey to these kinds of thoughts, a form of paranoia that he got from his mother; he recognised it in himself but was unable to eradicate it.

The man finished his cigarette and got to his feet. 'Let's go,' he said, and started walking, Malone following with his hands stuffed in his pockets. His fears about the air quality proved unfounded; evidently there was ventilation, or else no one smoked on the lower floors.

'Can I ask a question?' said Malone.

'Go ahead.'

'Will I be able to meet him?'

'If you want.'

'When?'

'Tonight, tomorrow.'

Malone was surprised by the man's offhand manner. He had been in Malone's position not so long ago, had he forgotten how it felt? The uncertainty, the fear, the sense that things might not turn out as you hoped? An unbearable situation.

After a quarter of an hour they reached the basement. It was dark outside; a few lights flickered in the distance. They looked like gas lamps to Malone.

'The grid's down,' the man explained. 'They're working on it, but until they fix it this is all we've got.'

He led Malone across the bitumen to the car. The night was silent as an empty house. Malone couldn't say if he was hot or cold since his hands and face seemed incapable of registering anything other than the simplest stimuli. He would have liked to examine his face in a mirror to reassure himself that it was still the same.

'That's it?' Malone said as they walked side by side. 'I don't have to sign anything?'

'I told you, we don't keep records.'

'Then how do you know who's here?'

'Everyone's here.'

They pulled onto the highway and headed west, their headlights opening a path through the darkness. From time to time Malone caught glimpses of people walking along the road; they appeared in flashes, like trees or posts illuminated by lightning, then retreated into obscurity.

'Who are they?' Malone asked.

'People,' the man said.

'But where are they going?'

'The same place we're going.'

'Shouldn't we pick them up?'

'All of them?' the man asked.

'We could take a few.'

'And what about the rest? Just leave them on the highway?'

'Isn't that what we're doing anyway?'

'I can't take some and leave the others; how would it look? Besides, if I stop the car, we'll be mobbed. Then you can forget about meeting anyone.'

Malone sighed and sat back in his seat. He strained his eyes, trying to penetrate the gloom. In the middle distance, maybe a few hundred metres from the road, he could make out a series of shapes at regular intervals.

'Are they buildings?'

The man nodded.

'What kind?'

'I don't know; I only come this way at night.'

Malone reached for the glove compartment.

'Don't open that,' the man said sharply.

'Why, what's in it?'

'If I wanted you to know I wouldn't have told you not to open it.'

Again, Malone was impressed by the man's logic and imperious tone. You wouldn't want to make an enemy of someone like that. From the way his hands gripped the steering wheel, Malone guessed he would be extremely powerful. On the other hand, sometimes big men were soft, their size making strength unnecessary.

'Will I have to work?' asked Malone.

'They'll find something for you to do.'

'I was a musician before the accident,' he said.

The man looked straight ahead as if he hadn't heard.

'I said I was a musician once,' Malone repeated.

'I heard you.'

'You don't have anything to say?'

'What do you want me to say?'

'I don't know. I thought it might interest you.'

'Two nights ago I picked up a soldier, a young guy. The whole trip he talked to me about his time in the army. I wasn't interested but I let him talk because he felt the need. If you feel the need to talk, go ahead, but don't expect me to be interested. You people come out here full of stories you think no one's ever heard before.'

Malone frowned. Later he would say to himself, nothing ever changes, and there would be regret in his voice (or the thought of his voice since he was alone) but also acceptance, a kind of tired recognition not unlike what the old entertainers felt in their twilight years when they sat backstage contemplating their ruined faces in the mirror and said: the show must go on.

They passed a military convoy heading in the opposite direction. Malone turned in his seat to watch them. 'Where are they going?' he asked.

'How would I know?'

'Is there fighting here?'

'There's fighting everywhere,' the man said, turning to look at Malone. 'It surprises you, doesn't it?'

'Nobody told us it would be like this.'

The man smiled. 'You believed what they told you?'

'Not all of it, no, but yes I thought … I thought it would be different.'

'It's not, it's just more of the same.'

'So what happened before …'

'Doesn't matter.'

'And those who did wrong?'

'Forgotten.'

'So there's no justice?'

'These things you're talking about, they're just words, they don't mean anything.'

'And that doesn't bother you?'

'I have no say in it.'

Malone rested his head against the window and felt the glass tremble in his ear. It was as if his whole being was vibrating like the string of a mandolin. The glass, the road and Malone himself all merged into a single entity, a single experience, moving steadily along an indeterminate span of time.

They pulled over at a service station to fill up. The gauge said half-full but it was broken, the man explained, he went by distance, writing the numbers down in a notebook he kept in the console.

It was while he waited for the man to come out of the bathroom that Malone realised there was no moon in the sky. Things like this make all the difference.

Someone somewhere was playing music. A rippled-piano and lonely-trumpet serenade. The source was a mystery to Malone as he ran his eyes along the line of cars, thinking of drive-ins and radios. Other memories came. Standing outside a concert hall listening to Beethoven in the rain; the music of department stores and elevators pumped into cabins from unseen speakers. While he sat there he noticed a small black object on the windscreen: somehow the fly had managed to get inside the car.

The man returned, walking with a slight limp. Something had happened in the bathroom but Malone didn't ask what it was.

The last hour passed quickly. They entered the city around ten. The place looked rundown. There were broken windows and people queuing outside soup kitchens. But the power was back on and the billboards shone like stars. Among the advertisements for toothpaste and office furniture were giant portraits of a man with blank eyes and a harelip.

'Is that him?' asked Malone.

The man nodded.

They drove through crowded streets, Malone watching it all from behind the glass. He saw familiar faces, people he'd seen in pictures and newsreels. An actress from another era was sitting at an outdoor table with men in gabardine suits. Three blocks away the killer Wassermann, his head still bandaged, leant against a lamppost smoking a cigarette.

The man drove on to the compound. It looked like a fort or one of those ancient cities that have been buried under the sand. The man showed his papers at the gate and the guards waved them through.

They waited in a foyer with a marble dog and multi-coloured walls. It was almost midnight when they were shown into the main room. There, in the centre, was a tiny little man with blank eyes and a harelip. He was sitting on the floor, playing with a rubber ball. When the newcomers entered, he looked up briefly then returned to his ball.

Malone didn't know what to say; he couldn't grasp exactly what he was seeing. After a moment he gathered himself together. 'Excuse me,' he began.

'You're wasting your time,' the man said. 'He's an idiot, he can't understand a word you're saying.'

In defence of the bodhran
Leonie Needham

Can you hear the bodhrans, Tommy?
'Nooo, t'ank God,' said he
And he an Irishman an' all
Not responding to the call
Not responding to the beat
The beat that came from winnowing wheat
From Spanish heat, the beat, the beat
I worry for his soul
Your strings may tell a story, Tommy
But the story's not complete
Without the beat of the bodhran
Your song is lost to the wind
That rhythmic beat, that primitive sound
As the tipper hits the skin
The drum is the heartbeat of the song
Now let the story begin
Listen for the beat of the bodhran, Tommy
A steady comforting sound
The drummer's hand is moving fast
Watch the wrist, the flick and twist
Painting on the song lines
And the drum loves bein' kissed
The whispering grows to a galloping roar
In a rhythm we dare not resist
Be mindful of the bodhran, Tommy
As you play your jigs and reels
Hypnotic, erotic, it won't be still
Till your soul begins to heal
Till it captures the beat in all our hearts
And sparks a light in our eyes
That is the strength of the bodhran, Tommy
It's beating the time of our lives
Can you hear the bodhrans, Tommy?

The bicycle
Daniel Harper

It is Juma's turn with the hoe. He moves slowly; sweat beads on his skin. Bento Ngunga, his father, is behind him in the furrow, breaking the clods of dry earth with his hands. Juma is almost a man now; his back is muscular and his arms are wiry, like his father's. Working together like this they inch forward, preparing the field to be sown.

Bento's own father would say to him: *There are no shortcuts to the top of a palm tree.* Bento tries to keep this wisdom alive by teaching it to his children. He wants them to grow to be wise, so he collects knowledge like this whenever he can. Standing to stretch his back, Bento looks out to the chalk-white mountaintop in the distance and the dry hills that roll down to the edge of the fields.

A little later, the others appear on the path. Otelo is nearly as tall as Bento's shoulders now. On his head he carries a yellow drum full of water from the well. Muhuwa has the large can and her small rag doll. Her baby sister is on her back in the folds of her capulana. The corners of the blue cloth are tied diagonally across her chest.

Otelo's rubber sandals have worn through. He has cracks in his heels and there is dry blood between the toes of one foot. Juma's sandals are too big and Bento has none of his own to give him. Bento knows he could use some of the money in the small can to buy him a new pair. He worries he is making a mistake by not doing so. When he thinks about it, a burning flares in his stomach like a hot coal.

Unburdening themselves, they sit together under the branches of the shade tree. Bento picks up baby Maria and holds her high above his head. This is the moment he has waited for the whole morning. He hears her laughter and looks up to see her smiling face in front of the branches and the points of light between them.

Being around his children enlivens Bento, and again he tells them about the bicycle. *It is shiny. It gleams in all parts, from the mirror on the handlebar to the metal guard over the chain; from the yellow frame to the red reflective plate behind the seat. It has a bell that rings out like the call to church on Sunday. Imagine what we can do with this machine.*

The boys keep listening, resting on their elbows. Maria totters off behind the tree trunk, giggling as Muhuwa chases after her, both with big round bellies. A solitary breeze blows through like a gift from God.

Imagine, Otelo, if you set out at dawn, with this bicycle you could be back before breakfast. You could carry twice as much water with half the effort. And the other two could stay at home. Juma, imagine how easily we could carry cassava flour to the market. We could take it to the city market and bring home twice the money. And the sesame. No more dealing with Acúrsio. That alone is worth the price. Juma smiles. He knows Acúrsio well, with narrow eyes and hands that you must watch in every exchange.

Bento recounts all this because he wants them to remain hopeful. Their sesame crop was destroyed in a gale, and all they have left to sell are the few bushels drying in the yard – their field of yellow flowers had been wiped out overnight. Bento no longer carves his wooden figures: there is no-one to buy them here in his wife's village. And he and Juma share a troubling secret. During the last months they have been digging up the cassava roots earlier and earlier. They've been able to save a little money this way but they both know that soon there won't be enough food left in the ground to sustain them.

That night, before bed, Bento takes the small can from its hiding place under the stone. He counts the roll of notes and it soothes him to see it all still there. Now that he's sold the book they are over halfway to their goal.

It was the only book they had ever owned, a leather-bound Bible given as a wedding present by the parish. On receiving it, Bento gently opened the cover to marvel at page after page of beautiful printed scripture. It was written entirely in Makhuwa. When they were blessed with Juma, they hoped he might one day use it to learn the written words of their language. Perhaps he could have taught the others. All the dreams they had for their children … now that book is gone.

In this part of Mozambique, north of the Zambezi, they say a fool has many days. Bento wonders if it's the foolish road he's chosen. He lies awake on his thin blanket; he can feel the dirt on his heel through a hole. The little ones breathe softly and slowly at his side. He stares at the thatch above him and thinks about Otelo's foot and about the rains. His mind drifts above the roof to the star-filled heavens and he worries about the sesame harvest. Everything they have, their whole existence, has been gambled on those bushels in the yard. As his mind slips to dreaming he floats in the night sky, clear with a million diamond pinpoints. A sharp picture comes into focus as he flies, the object that they risk it all for – the image of a yellow bicycle.

***

On Sunday after church, Bento goes with Vicente, his wife's father, to visit her. They walk through the village to the hill behind and stop in the presence of the baobab tree. Two white crosses stand in the earth before them – one large, one small. Vicente lays some dried flowers before the large one.

They stand for a time and then the old man turns his searching eyes on Bento. *How are you?* Coming from Vicente this is not a greeting, rather it is a question.

God provides for me and my family.

He has noticed Bento is not himself for he says to him: *A man does not run among thorns for no reason. Either he is chasing a snake or a snake is chasing him.*

Bento needs to tell him he does not want to be thought a fool. *It is not a snake*

I am chasing, it is a bicycle.

Vicente's eyes probe again, then he turns back to the crosses. Bento knows he's thinking about what happened. The health post is far.

Vicente returns from a place in his heart a long way from where they stand. *I have some good news,* he says. He hands Bento several folded banknotes and a pair of small rubber sandals. *A white person visited our village, and I sold it.*

It had been years since anyone had bought one of Bento's carvings, and never at such a price.

When Bento tells him after dinner, Juma sits forward, arms hugging his shins. For the first time it's actually possible. They linger together by the fire and they laugh, eyes shining with thoughts of what this might bring. Flames leap into the cold night air.

The flour we could carry, Juma says. *How much could we get at the city market?*

More than at Namiroa.

How long to the well by bicycle?

Not far.

To the city market? All the way to Nampula?

His father smiles.

A burning log collapses into coals and a silence falls over them. They both know that without a decent yield of sesame seeds it will all be for nothing.

***

When the time to harvest the sesame arrives, every blade of grass in the village is crisp and dry. The surrounding hills are the colour of dry straw. Together they go to the field – Bento, Juma and Otelo. Juma spreads the blanket beneath the shade tree, folding it diagonally to cover the holes. Otelo lays the empty water drum beside it and they set to work.

The brittle sesame bushels are bound together with ties made from palm fronds. Juma carries them over his shoulder in fours and fives and lays them in a pile. Bento and Otelo stand each bushel on the blanket in turn and run a stick down it to break open the cracked pods. God has heard their prayers for rain. Sesame seeds explode onto the blanket.

When Otelo cracks the last of the pods and the blanket is covered with seeds, a crow arrives. Bento hears the ruffle of his wings as he settles above them in the shade tree. Another joins him. Soon a third and eventually a murder perches above them, squawking and coveting the crop like a dozen thieves of the sky. Bento pulls the corners of the blanket across but it only partially covers the pile. He stands beside it, fists clenched, surveying the branches above.

The first crow swoops. Bento lunges at him but he's not fast enough to stop him stealing a beak full of seeds. Soon another and another fly in arcs, swarming and whittling away the pile. The two boys shift handful after handful of seeds into the yellow drum, moving furiously to save what they can. Bento's knuckles are white. *All of our labours, all of the sacrifices we have made — we have suffered much for this pile of seeds.* He catches one of the filthy birds by the wing and wrings its neck.

The other crows now remain on the spindly branches. They shift from one foot to the other. He hears them cry out in anger. Is it for their lost brethren? Or do they cry for themselves? Because these crows feel something they need desperately for survival is slipping away from them.

When the last handful of seed rests in the drum it's lighter than usual. Juma hangs his head on the way home and his father walks with his hand on the boy's shoulder. It will all depend on the exchange with Acúrsio tomorrow and this troubles Bento. He wrestles with his thoughts through the afternoon. Finally, he decides to visit his wife's father for advice.

Vicente crouches on his haunches in front of his hut. Bento crouches beside him, both of them looking out to the hills. The old man smokes a rolled cigarette with the smooth and purposeful movements of a master craftsman. He considers the problem as it was put to him: *If I take an unknown weight to Acúrsio, I risk being deceived on the turn of his scales. If I pay for the seeds to be weighed, I risk not having enough money for the bicycle.*

Vicente draws deeply, allows the smoke to roll over his upper lip and into his nostrils before he exhales a milky stream. After a time he says this: *A snake you can see does not bite.*

It is true what they say, Vicente is indeed a wise man.

***

The following day, on the way to the market at Namiroa they stop at a roadside stall. Bento hands one of his notes to a thin woman in exchange for a piece of paper with a number and the letter K. When he gives it to Juma, his son tells him they have twelve kilograms of seed. Folding the paper carefully, Bento puts it in his breast pocket. There are blisters now under his ankle on one side and behind his heel on the other. The leather shoes he wears belong to one of his neighbours.

They come to the part of the road where the cars drive. A truck rumbles past and dust rises like two coiling serpents behind it. In the distance the mountains are green, with huge stones at the highest peak leaning in to confer like elders around the fire. Unseasonable dark clouds gather overhead and there is a growing thickness of the air. The day becomes heavier the closer they get to the market.

Acúrsio has cheated them before. When Juma returned from his trip with the last sesame harvest, they discovered there was a note missing from the money he received. The following day when his father made the journey to confront Acúrsio, the trader denied it. *Do you even know what these numbers mean?* Acúrsio pointed to the symbols on a banknote while the traders at the next stalls laughed at the poor farmer. They looked at Acúrsio without really seeing him, and they laughed like Bento was not even there.

As they walk along Bento feels his breast pocket. The paper is still there. Today they will not be cheated. *To fight a lion you must be a lion* – the thought remains in his mind as they near the market.

When they arrive it's raining. Women wearing brightly coloured capulanas carry woven baskets on their heads, men bustle with bags of goods to be sold and children run weaving through the throng. As they approach the stall, Acúrsio appears over the crowd; he sits up high on a large hessian sack. He wears a blue shirt made from shiny material and has gold chains around his neck. Bento notices his tongue flash out across his bottom lip. With his narrow eyes and licking tongue he is like a cunning lizard. They wait patiently, heavy drops beating down on them. Acúrsio remains dry under the canvas awning.

Finally their turn comes. *Good afternoon.* Acúrsio holds out his limp hand, which Bento shakes. A loose gold watch hangs from the wrist. *Good afternoon.* Acúrsio's skin is so smooth his arm looks like it would slip right out of your grasp. *What can I do for you?* He does not remember them. *Sesame seeds? Oh no, not much demand for those at the moment. I cannot offer much I'm afraid.*

Juma fixes the price. It is lower than last time, but the boy is good with numbers and he knows this amount will be enough.

They tip their seeds into the large dish for weighing. The burning gnaws in Bento's stomach as he watches the red needle move across the numerals. It wobbles before stopping. He looks to his son who shakes his head. Juma's eyes plead with him.

This is not right. Bento pulls out the piece of paper and waves it at Acúrsio. *I had this weighed this morning. It is twelve kilograms.*

I'm sorry but your scales are inaccurate. This is only ten, Acúrsio says.

No, this cannot be. Those waiting around them jostle impatiently.

It is certainly correct, sir. Here is your money. Please, move along.

A rude woman says something behind them.

A lion inside Bento roars. *No sir. We will not be moving until we have the correct weight!*

Acúrsio turns to the next stall holder who obliges by removing his own weighing dish and passing it over to him. Acúrsio stands and transfers the seeds with some effort. As he places it on the neighbouring scales Bento wonders whether Acúrsio might actually be correct. *Is it my own paper that is wrong?*

His stomach knots again as the red needle moves. It vacillates. It stops on a number. He looks to Juma again. *What's it say, boy?*

Juma grins from ear to ear. *Twelve. It says twelve.*

***

The rain has stopped by the time Bento coasts out of the market, the sun reaching its fingers down through breaks in the clouds. He can't believe it's really him on this bicycle; he rides along as if in a dream. The bicycle is just as he described it – shining, yellow, new. With the uncertainty of a novice, he sways to and fro, but he manages to stay on, and with God's grace avoids colliding with any pedestrians. Out of the market and along the side of the road, he glides beneath the trees. He is so happy he reaches up to hit the dripping branches with his fist, and cool water buckets down on him and his new machine. To Bento, it feels like flying.

The trip that took most of the day on foot is over very quickly. Poor Juma will have to walk all this way back. On the street of their village women emerge from their homes and children sprint from huts and fields to chase the machine. They all follow him home. Otelo and Muhuwa didn't know about the plans that day and they survey their new possession wide-eyed. They pour over the frame, feeling the smooth cold metal, testing the ring of the bell and smelling the golden oil from the chain on their fingers. Baby Maria hears her big brother and sister laughing; she echoes them with a little burst of her own. Otelo and Muhuwa hold hands and spin around her in a circle.

Half of the village has now arrived at their hut. There is singing and ululation. There is dancing. His wife's father pats Bento on the back and produces a bottle of palm wine. The farmer recounts his story, their hard-won savings, their windfall, the thieving crows and the cheating lizard at the market. He tries to think of some knowledge to share, something a wise man would use to finish his tale. He says this: *Waphwany'* eétthú, khumphwánya veekháu. If you achieve something, you do not achieve it alone.

He feels indebted to them all and he's alive with the possibilities of life. By selling their cassava flour in the city they will begin to rebuild, Otelo will have time to work with them in the field and they will re-sow the sesame. With their new profits Bento decides he will buy some sandals. He will expand their fields and begin saving again.

When Juma arrives later, Bento explains the new plans. *We will pull ourselves up by our bootstraps*, he says. *This time we will save for a motorcycle.*

Tangled
Stefan Dubczuk

A handful of thumbs among
a spray of frayed, tightly-knotted laces; oh,
um, and some un-graspable phrases;
two scuffed, hard-nosed shoes tangled
at the tongues.
Incomprehension webs
his cheesy smile like a child messy
with spaghetti – as I, now his parent, somehow
loosen, untwist and untie, part
the wreckage, loop two limp hearts,
tug loose ends, bow and gesture:
Ta Da! Magic! A trick of which
he never tires.
He forgets remembering –
a slow erosion – the tentative fingering
of rudimentary English through the refracted
black and white and red linguistic prism of Poland,
the Ukraine and Russia; then Yugoslavia;
and that final German solution
for lost words – all of those soulless *-isms*
that stamp a youthful throat.
And
should he choose some obtuse tangled
language from his distant past, instead
of his usual *what are you doing
next week?* still I would chorus, our laughter
soaring into guffaws loosening rafters, falling,
gliding into our Friday early-hour ritual,
tongue-tied in unison.

The life in the attic
Kerstin Lindros

With a flick of his wrist, Walter dislodged a white thread from the thick fabric of the stone-grey uniform coat. His hands gently stroked down the length of the sleeves. He spotted a dog hair just above the hem and reached for the lint brush next to the mirror inside the wardrobe door. 'Hasso!' Walter cried out, pointing his finger at the big German shepherd, now under the old table that served as his desk. He rushed over, chuckled and rubbed Hasso's head, tousling the dog's long hair. Shuffling back over to the wardrobe, his eyes briefly met those of *Genosse* H in the old portrait on the wall. He had stepped back and was scrutinising the coat all over, nodding his approval, when the screechy horn of the postman's bike catapulted him back into the present. He quickly placed the hanger back on the rail, closed the wardrobe door and left the partition that had become his office in the attic.

Walter hurried down the creaky staircase and thought about insulation. Up there, the temperature hadn't gone below twenty-five degrees all night. He had been reading until late by the light of a bedside lamp on a long extension cord, and his large body had melted into the tatty winged armchair. Now he was rubbing his sore neck. Had Rosemarie seen, she would have given him a lecture on poor sleep habits and their consequences for his wellbeing. But she was working the night shift at the hospital this week, again.

At the kitchen table he read the paper. Drugs, abuse and unemployment; protesters in the city, calling themselves Patriotic Europeans against Islamisation *… That's what we've come to in twenty-five years. What a fiasco,* he thought. *Once we were all equal, all had jobs. Now we are at the mercy of the powerful — they had to push until the Wall toppled. The lure of glitz and glamour … Schmucks.*

He reassembled the pages and tossed the paper onto the kitchen bench for Rosemarie; she'd rage if she found the paper in disorder. He stuck a pod into the Nespresso machine and dropped some bread into the toaster. Outside the window he saw a bluetit fly off with a caterpillar in its beak, off to the pine tree to bring breakfast to its mate tending to the nest. In the early years, Walter used to wait to have breakfast with Rosemarie after her night shift.

Rosemarie had found it easier to part with the little red Party book and cross over into the bright new world, but she always knew Walter would need more time. At first she still came to meetings with the old comrades. She used to say the past was the past. Everyone needed a fair go. Needed time. She understood. Now Rosemarie didn't have much to say to Walter anymore, at least not much beyond 'don't forget the rubbish' or 'my car needs oil'. But they were doing okay.

Comrade Richard had been right about women only the day before, when the old brigade had met over a bottle of Lunikoff vodka. Most in the troop had new wives. Their old wives couldn't do without the perks; they went on strike and finally defected. They had no principles. They never belonged. But the men had pledged loyalty, to each other and to the institution. Walter was lucky. Rosemarie was a stayer. A keeper. Richard was lucky, too. He'd found his new gem in 1994, but that was no surprise. She had been an accomplished leader, back in the day. She had worked in Recruitment.

Walter had tried hard to adjust. Bought a little house in a village not far from the city, donned a wig and grew a beard for a fresh start. After restocking shelves at the supermarket he had worked himself up into car sales, but then he lost his job to a young lad.

Many of the comrades, especially the younger ones, had stumbled into secure jobs in security, or insurance, or as private eyes and debt collectors. Their skills were timeless. Richard retired three years ago but was still called in to his old workplace sometimes to get into people's heads and force their innermost thoughts into surrender, to chisel away at their protective shells. Recently he kept asking a guy the same question again and again, and every time the poor sod repeated exactly the same answer. A great performance, but what a classic. He stumbled. It was a well-proven method back then at the Firm. Richard destroyed him. *Comrade, you've still got it.*

Now he heard Rosemarie's car. He straightened the roses in the vase on the kitchen table and placed the paper next to the vase. He had picked the flowers up at the service station last night after the meeting in Richard's cave. One of the buds was slightly limp, and Walter tried to support it gently with his right hand, but to no avail.

Rosemarie walked in with shopping bags. She ignored the roses and began unpacking and putting away the groceries. She didn't buy into Walter's chitchat.

'I'm off to work then,' Walter said.

Rosemarie nodded after a moment of silence.

'No goodbye, eh?' he asked.

'I wish you didn't creep around in the suburbs, on buses and trains, and report—'

'People know the rules. They know the rules. When you're off work on certificate—'

Rosemarie shook her head. 'I thought you'd changed.'

'I found a job.' He threw his arms up. 'You wanted me to get a job.'

She glared at him. 'Yeah. An honest one.'

'Don't keep bringing up the past.'

'You move on then,' she chided him. 'The old days are gone. Move on,' she muttered as she plastered jam on her toast at the bench.

Walter had already left. The front door crashed into its lock; the hinges of the gate creaked. Rosemarie stood at the window and watched him reverse the Lada out onto the road.

***

A rainy autumn came. During the cold, dark and damp season, Rosemarie dried the washing upstairs, pegging the garments to the web of rope that criss-crossed the attic just above head height. She never approached the office chamber at the other end. It was a deal they had made when Walter started setting up office. Her world, his world – it worked.

When she opened the attic door and Walter was in, streaks of light flooded across the floor through the gaps between the wooden slats of the walls. His chamber was the partition next to the one that housed old furniture, suitcases and boxes. From there, the little TV and the old couch had recently made their way into the chamber. During the past months, Rosemarie had watched Walter carry many parcels and boxes up the stairs. Now, she often saw a glimmer, a black and white flicker, and heard the crackly sound of *Genosse* H's mumbling preachy voice. One day a bulky rectangular box was delivered when Walter was out, and when he came home, Rosemarie quipped, 'This one's big enough for a body.'

He had thrown his head back and chuckled.

After much drilling and sawing, more and more cables and wires snaked out from the chamber and disappeared into the attic floor. Sometimes a telephone now rang upstairs. Every Friday the entire house reeked of diesel. She remembered the old roll of linoleum Walter had carried up with Richard some weeks ago. He must have been waxing it, like they did in the old days. One day, cigar smoke and a whiff of vodka streamed from the chamber and lingered long after he'd left. Still, Rosemarie didn't approach. They had a deal. Even when he wasn't upstairs, the chamber exhaled its stale breath through the narrow gaps in the wall. But more often than not, Walter was in his chamber now.

***

One afternoon in early December, it was almost four o'clock when darkness was about to creep in. Despite the icy draft that whistled through the tiny gaps in the roof, the attic was Walter's sanctuary. He flicked the little blow heater on and walked over to the window to watch two bluetits prise sunflower seeds out of the lard in the feeder he had hung from a bracket outside the attic window. A warm smile spread across his face. The feeder swung back and forth and the birds had to hold on tight. The lines on his forehead smoothed and his lips became soft. Walter felt for the birds that stayed during the long and cold winters, especially once it would begin to snow. The bluetits were loyal birds. They didn't shy away when the cold set in. They were resilient. Principled. Determined. Hasso barked at the flutter outside. Walter raised his palm. 'Shush now.' Hasso obeyed.

In a gust of wind some dust blew off a beam onto his book-covered desk. He eyed the Lenin bust and wiped it with his sleeve to make the large bronze forehead shine again. He looked up at the roof and made plans for a ceiling. He was saving up now that he was earning money again, even if it wasn't much.

Walter strutted to the old wardrobe and opened its door. He looked into the mirror and laid his hand upon his coarse brown hair. He slid the toupee off and tossed it onto the desk. Then he grabbed the heavy coat hanger with his uniform and hung it from the top of the wardrobe door as Hasso brushed past.

'Hasso!' he shouted. He raised his fist and took a leap toward the dog. 'On your bed!'

Hasso trudged to his pillow, head down and tail pulled in between the legs. The dog was his closest ally. He had earned his stripes. Downstairs, Walter treated him like the child he never had. Hasso sat on the corner bench at the table and he slept on the marital bed. But the chamber demanded discipline.

He boiled the kettle and made himself a pot of tea. He inhaled deeply – the scent of sweetened black tea took him back to the barracks.

After sipping some of the strong brew he slipped his arms into the sleeves of the coat, pulled it up over his shoulders and closed the shiny aluminium buttons. It was still tight, but he could close it again. The eat-half diet was the strategy that would lead to success. He patted the silver braid on his shoulders and the bling on the left side of his chest. He stood erect. He mounted the visor hat on his almost bald head. Up here, he was the Major again. He poured himself some vodka and downed it. Then another, a larger one.

Footsteps downstairs made Hasso stand up at the door. Walter hadn't heard Rosemarie's car. He stripped down to his tracksuit, threw the coat onto the couch and rushed out. In the stillness, the bolt scraped into its socket.

When he stepped into the kitchen reeking of vodka, Rosemarie turned away. She ignored the fresh service station roses on the table and continued peeling carrots, staring at the thin peelings that curled towards her with every stroke. From opposite the window where he sat to read the paper, Walter saw Mrs Schultz's Christmas tree glowing warmly in her backyard. Last week he had watched the old woman decorate it slowly, in her thick steel-blue cardigan and a woolly scarf wrapped around her neck and shoulders, two boxes with lights and ornaments on the seat of her walker. It had taken her almost an hour before she waved him out to help her fasten the last pieces up high. Walter liked Mrs Schultz. She was always kind to him when he dropped in with her weekly shopping. She often told him about her son, a toolmaker. She was proud of her son.

Walter looked around the room and turned to Rosemarie. 'No angels, candles and stars this year, Rosie?' he asked.

'What's the point? You're never home.'

After a quiet dinner Rosemarie disappeared into the bedroom.

***

The next afternoon Walter came home from his field work with a floral Christmas arrangement. 'Hasso!' He switched the Nespresso machine on and called for Rosemarie. He walked through the entire house before arriving in the bedroom. The beds were decked out with fresh linen; her wardrobe was empty.

He stood next to the bed, hunched and frozen. After minutes he straightened. With his jaw still clenched, he climbed the staircase to the attic and lugged a large rectangular box down into the lobby. There, he assembled the parts of an old mannequin near the entrance door. Then he brought down his uniform and draped it around the mannequin before crowning it with his visor hat. In the kitchen, he made himself coffee and read the paper, shaking his head at the world.

Smokers outside hospital doors

Anna Ryan-Punch

'Christ, Dad was heavy. Must've had his wallet in there with him.'

***

Sam kicked one shoe against the other. He drew back his shoulders as hard as he could, then let them curl forwards again. One hand smeared his fringe across to one side. When he glanced up for the twentieth time, the wall of relatives still drifted in a haze of smoke. His family coiled in a clutch, squeezing snakes of grey fumes into the air. Sam eyed the heavily capitalised sign: 'No Smoking Within 10 Metres Of Hospital Air Intake Vents'. His family wasn't the only one puffing too close to the slats; there were lots of quiet smokers. Pregnant women in wheelchairs disobeyed the warnings on the packs. Emaciated teenagers ignored their wrung-out mothers. Young men with faces like white bread and heroin pinched out a last gasp of freedom. Old blokes who looked perfectly healthy sucked away while their wives cried quietly behind them. The smokers outside the hospital doors were a statement. They had nothing left to lose but they didn't have freedom.

'I don't think he's got much left in him now.' Helen wasn't a smoker. She snapped chewing gum around her teeth like a rubber band.

Carol drew a deep draft from her cigarette. 'Have you told him?' She paused. The small orange light in her hand quivered and then steadied.

'No.' Helen chewed faster. 'Not my place.'

Sam listened. He guessed he was hearing something new, something he wasn't meant to understand. Maybe that wasn't quite right. He wasn't meant to hear it at all. As this thought arose, Sam's movements ground to a halt. He slipped into his mother's shadow outside the glass hospital doors. He slowed his breathing and concentrated. He pretended he was a rising column of smoke, as anonymous as any of the fags being whittled down outside the Warrnambool Base Hospital.

'You've told him she's been in contact.' Sam's mother was the first to speak. So soft; almost an apology. Elizabeth almost never spoke quietly. Her foghorn voice was notorious.

'Yeah, I told him,' said Carol. Her voice cracked like a biscuit. She scrubbed one wrist along the base of her nose. 'Last time he was awake, and understood … was understanding us. Couple of weeks. Couple of weeks ago.' She blew heavily through her nostrils. Leftover smoke curled up. 'She wanted to meet, wanted to see him.' Carol waved a hand through the grey air. 'I said it wasn't a good idea. I mean, what's he going to say, and what's she going to get out of it anyway at this stage …' her voice faltered.

Elizabeth slid in close to Carol, snaked an arm around her hips. 'It's all right. It's all right, love, really. It's all right.' Her voice still soft.

Sam stayed in his mother's shadow, even though it meant moving a little to follow her. He kept his breath steady and watched the sisters form a triangle in front of him. Elizabeth put her arm around Carol. Carol put her arm around Helen. Helen put her arm around Elizabeth. Sam watched their ribcages draw in and out as one. Two cigarettes quivered at half-mast, held away from clothing.

***

His urine bag was dark brown, towards the end. Dark in a way you couldn't ignore. Sam relegated himself to the back of the hospital room. He pressed his thin shoulders into the smooth white corner of the wall. In these moments where nothing happened, he was bored enough to be angry.

I'm not the sum of this family, he thought. Just because there's so many of them and they can't deal with it. I've got a father, too. He's not dying, he's at work. *Theirs* is dying.

Sam had recently learned the phrase 'elephant in the room'. The beast was reflected in the eyes of everyone in his family. Three sisters, three brothers and a giant invisible pachyderm wilting on grey sheets. He breathed through his mouth to try to drown out the smell of his grandfather, though it would still be lingering in the back of his throat when he got to the car.

'*Good* morning, how *are* we today?'

A nurse, bristling with grotesque amounts of toast and teabags slapped into thick-rimmed cups. Sam reached for one. Nothing is comfortable in hospitals, he thought. Even the holes in cup-handles are too small for normal human fingers. The brew scalded the roof of his mouth. It burned like UHT milk always makes tea burn. The toast looked like it had been microwaved for a month. Sam's mother glanced at him a few times but looked away each time he met her eyes.

***

The nurse drew the sheet up halfway. 'I'll leave you with him for a while.' She backed out of the room, and the family eyed her white uniform like it was a life-raft floating away. Then everyone's gaze fell upon the old man. Sam tilted his head slightly and re-imagined him as The Body. They hadn't removed the urine bag yet. It was almost black. The oil burner didn't mask the smell any more.

'Oh, Sam.' His mother's voice erased his carefully constructed detachment.

'Mum?' said Sam.

She wrapped her arms up around him. He was taller than her already. 'This is too hard on you, all this,' she said loudly.

Sam kept his eyes down. At least she was loud again. 'It's okay, Mum.'

Eventually he returned his mother's embrace, but his eyes slid across to Carol. She gnawed the skin around her fingernails. Helen snaked an arm around her waist, and she closed her fingers on Helen's. Sam shut his eyes, just for a few seconds. He wasn't meant to know about whatever it was. Which worked fine, because he didn't know what it was.

The room hovered in warm death for a few minutes. Then the door pressed open and a perky bob popped through the bright crack.

'How are you all going, then?' the nurse whispered loudly. 'Would you like some breakfast? Can make it all a bit easier, have a bit of toast, you know?'

They froze in the weak morning light. Helen spoke first. 'Thanks,' she said, 'but we'll just get the tea from the kitchen.' The nurse drew back her turtle-head from the door-frame, and Sam noticed for the first time that there were men in the room too. He glared at his mother, Helen and Carol for a moment. Then he swung his head to take in his three uncles, standing with their chins raised in the corner. Finally, he frowned at his dead grandfather in the hospital bed.

One of the uncles spoke. 'Breakfast would've been good, Helen.'

Helen didn't make eye contact. 'Then order as much toast as you like.' She raised her eyes to the open-mouthed body on the sheets. 'I'd like to get some sleep,' she said to the old man. Her tone was violent but she turned gently, looked to her sisters. They flowed into step like a current behind her. At the last moment, Carol stopped and stretched her fingers out to Sam. It was a question, not a demand.

'Sweetheart?' Her hand was the fish he'd been casting for. He took it and let himself be drawn from the room. He stared at his mother's back as she padded up the hospital corridor and thought: It should have been her that stretched out her hand.

***

'I won't make a scene; I would just like to say a few words,' Carol frowned. Sam pretended to slide things around on his iPhone. He hadn't even turned the screen on.

Elizabeth cleared her throat. 'Do you think that it's the best thing for her, to hear so early on …' she trailed off. The three men and two women looked at Carol. Sam looked at his iPhone. Everyone's doing an awful lot of looking, he thought.

Finally, Des cleared his throat. 'You're not making a speech, Carol. Everyone who needs to know, knows already. We don't need all that dragged through in public, especially not at the funeral. I'll do the eulogy, Elizabeth can do the gospel reading, Peter can do the prayers of the faithful.'

Carol's mouth tightened. She glanced at her sisters, but both Helen and Elizabeth seemed to have found something fascinating about the rim of their coffee mugs. Carol's shoulders sank slowly. 'Don't call her "all that",' she murmured. 'She's a person, she's—'

'Little pitchers,' Des snapped. Sam's fingers paused over the blank iPhone screen. Carol left her sentence and her coffee unfinished. Elizabeth put her mug down on the table. It made the tiniest click, like a lid being put back on a tube of lipstick. The three sisters stood up as one.

'You can be a real bully sometimes, Des, you know that?' said Helen.

'Don't be ridiculous. I'm organising this the way Dad would have wanted it, and you know it. I'm not going to let Carol's hysteria embarrass everyone. That's her business and she can deal with it in private.' Des' thick-veined hand dwarfed his coffee mug. His shirt collar was too tight and his red farmer's neck looked out of place above a jacket and tie. It made him look like a bull in a suit.

Helen narrowed her eyes, 'It's all our business and you know it. Carol's done it the way Dad wanted it for twenty fucking years; don't you think she can stop now he's dead?'

Des sat completely still. 'Don't you swear at me. After the funeral, she can do whatever the bloody hell she likes.'

Sam's heart beat faster. He'd never seen them like this before. He swallowed. 'Mum?' It was meant to be quiet but the tension made his voice squeak.

The single word displaced the air in the room; some kind of fury was cut in half.

'Sam's got cricket practice,' said Elizabeth loudly. She smiled, after a fashion. 'We'll be off.'

***

For once, Sam didn't have his headphones on. He lay in the overly warm darkness of his bedroom and breathed along with the periodic whoosh of the central heating. The low voices of his parents drifted from the lounge room, just soft enough to be incomprehensible. He'd forgotten to close the venetians, and the streetlights spangled condensation on the window into diamonds. He tried to make sense of what he'd heard. There was someone that nobody would talk about and it had to do with Carol. There was definitely a great big elephant in the room with his family and it felt like it was about to stampede. Aunt Helen would stare down any beast, he thought, but his mother and Carol were more easily trampled. And what was that 'little pitchers' thing all about? He fumbled for his iPhone in the dark. It slipped from his half-grip like a bar of soap and he paused as it hit the floorboards. He was supposed to have no screen-time after 10 pm, and he'd been busted by the 'thunk' of a dropped phone in the past. But his parents' murmurs from the lounge room continued uninterrupted.

Sam Googled 'little pitchers' and the top search result explained the idiom. Oh, he thought. Great. Thanks, Uncle Des. Except that even if I do hear more than I'm supposed to, I *don't* understand it. Perhaps you could underestimate me a bit more in future.

A change in the tone of his parents' voices caught Sam's attention. His mother's voice rose sharply, then his father's bass undercurrent cut into her crescendo. She muted, abruptly. The low, resolving murmur began again.

Sam sat up slowly in bed, rested on his elbows. Blood thudded loudly in his ears and he tried to frown it into silence. He'd been on a hair-trigger of adrenaline since that morning's funeral arrangements. He forced his breaths to slow down.

After a minute, he filled his ribs with air once more and slid back the blankets. The iPhone clunked to the floor, again, but he merely raised his chin a little. Eyes down, he swept across his bedroom, toes first in an arc to the door. He swung it open with grace. The hall was slicked yellow in downlights. The sound of his parents' voices swelled and receded like quiet waves. Sam padded down the hallway, heel-toe, heel-toe. Arm in arm and row on row. The grade three choir song sprang to mind, unbidden and forceful. By the time he halted at the doorway, he had to clench his teeth to stop from shouting: 'Red her cheeks as rowans are, bright her eye as any star.'

He pressed one palm against the door-frame. The lounge room door was closed and a slow light, dull as custard, slid in a triangle from under the gap.

'... really would have kicked her out, you know,' Elizabeth's voice, carefully pressed down into softness. That made two times in the same week he'd heard her voice muted. Elizabeth continued, 'Completely out, no support. That was the condition. Out of the whole family, the whole town, the whole life that she knew. At seventeen. What would you have done? Or can't you even pretend to imagine?'

Sam's father's voice rumbled incomprehensibly. His deep bass always seemed incongruous with his five foot something.

Elizabeth answered whatever the question had been, 'On Facebook. She said she wanted, that she wanted ...' her voice dipped out of range briefly, then returned, '... coming to the funeral.'

The couch-springs squeaked as someone stood up. Sam stiffened outside the door then swept back along the corridor to his room. He pressed his door shut with barely a click. He opened up Notes on his phone and carefully poked at the touchscreen. *Seventeen*, he typed. *Would have kicked her out. Facebook. Coming to the funeral.* He curled his thumbs and then straightened them out slowly. *Carol. Seventeen. That was the condition.* He pressed the silver button on his phone and extinguished the room.

***

'Christ, Dad was heavy. Must've had his wallet in there with him.'

The three brothers roared with laughter. Sam tried to smile and shifted his weight from foot to foot. The relief of a smooth funeral service had erupted into the traditional family black humour and sly swigs from hip flasks. Sam suspected hip flasks only existed in country men's pockets and cigarette shops.

The hall was big, under-heated and strung with dusty pictures of the Queen. It had an electric pie-warming oven and industrial-sized metal teapots that were hefted in the meaty fists of CWA ladies. It felt like every school dance and wake that Sam had ever been to. His suit was polyester and clung damply to his armpits, knees and groin despite the chill in the hall. He'd grown in the last few months; the pant cuffs barely covered his ankles. He studied the pattern a knothole made in one of the floorboards. It looked like an owl or a big-eyed anime character.

Sam's uncles erupted into blaring hilarity at another joke. 'Pete, mate, when you're gunna move from bullshittin' to telling us the truth, could you let us know so we can tell how hard to laugh at ya?'

The room was divided into circles of men, circles of women, circles of the elderly and tumbling strings of children. Old people and kids can't be bothered separating into male and female. Helen, Carol, Elizabeth and a younger woman that Sam didn't know had formed a tight group at the funeral and still edged about the hall like the hems of their dresses were sewn together.

A red-armed woman in a bulging dress elbowed her way into the circle of men where Sam stood, using her plate of sandwiches like a ship's ice-breaker. She looked like Mrs Claus in floral acrylic.

'Got to keep your strength up, boys,' she huffed. 'More sangers?' Everyone reached toward the platter of white triangles.

'Good to be at a do where there's no vegos,' said a man Sam didn't know. 'Last week, after the Hudson funeral, half of it was bloody tomato and cheese. Even bloody eggs weren't on the cards – half of them allergic or some bullshit. So no curried egg, no vol-you-vents, none of that. I almost went to complain but Maureen had a go at me cos we didn't really know the deceased very well an' that—' Here he respectfully tipped an imaginary hat, '—but if the vegos can't just pick out the bits they don't like, like all the rest of us do …' He nodded. Nods were returned.

Sam took a sandwich and nervously shoved the whole triangle into his mouth. He'd seen red, pink and yellow bits in the filling, but all it tasted of was margarine. He swallowed it half-chewed.

An arm slid around Sam's shoulder. It was Helen. 'How you doing, love?' she said softly.

'All right,' said Sam. He shuffled a little closer to her.

'Come to sort out the men, have you, Hellraiser?' said Des.

Helen smiled but her grip on Sam's shoulder tightened. 'Good spread, boys?'

She addressed the circle of men as a whole.

'We've only got one boy here, Hellcat,' said Des.

'Oh, I don't know, I think there's still a few here get their pyjamas laid out for them.'

The circle of men roared bourbon breath. Des forced out a laugh like a punctuation mark. 'Swig of sanity, Helicopter?' He thrust his hip flask towards Helen. 'I've wiped it off, don't worry.'

Helen winked jovially. 'Wouldn't want to catch the family ailment, Des-perado.'

Des narrowed his eyes but his voice was warm and joking. 'Somebody's done something to you in your life, Helen, so that you don't trust anybody.'

Helen's voice rose comically as she delivered her punch line, 'It's not that I don't trust anybody, Des, it's just you!'

The circle of men exploded into shouts of laughter. Sam's ears caught exclamations of, 'Got one over you there!' and, '… the pants in this family!' as Helen steered him away from the circle.

'You okay?' she said.

'Yep,' said Sam. 'Ta, Helen.'

Helen led Sam past endless platters of post-funeral food. Lemon slice, jelly slice, hedgehog, Mars Bar slice, caramel slice – there was so much slice. Desiccated sandwich triangles were mostly the same margarine-flavoured variety that Sam had encountered. Soggy slices of tomato escaped their bready bookends and lay limply on beds of shredded lettuce. The vol-au-vent fillings had just started to form a skin on top and the top half of one passionfruit sponge had slid sideways across its cream centre. Enormous foil platters of chicken wings waved obscenely. Sam stared briefly at a tray of mini-muffins: horrible little Top Taste sultana cakes from the supermarket that had been decanted into individual patty pans to try to make them look homemade.

Helen guided Sam back to where Carol, Elizabeth and the mystery woman stood. They had settled in a corner of the room underneath a large wall-mounted oar.

'Hello, Sam love,' boomed Sam's mother. Sam relaxed a little at this. He was still uneasy with the new quiet mother he had witnessed recently.

Helen rubbed a hand across the top of Sam's shoulders: an unconscious, affectionate gesture. 'We've got someone we'd like you to meet. You've probably picked up some things over the last few weeks, you're no thickhead. And anyway, it's no secret any more, is it? It never should have been.' The four women nodded in unison.

Sam's eyes flicked from sister to sister, and then to the younger woman. 'Um, hi,' he said. He rubbed at one ear with the flat of his hand.

'Hi, Sam,' said the woman warmly. She was dressed in muted colours, like most of the women, but her dress hung a little more cleanly, was cut a little more impressively than theirs.

City, Sam thought.

Helen continued, 'Sam, this is Eva. She's family, she's Carol's daughter.'

Everything Sam had already half-known slid quietly into place, like a headphone jack into a socket. The music rang out clear and true. Carol. Seventeen. Would have kicked her out. She's family, she's Carol's daughter.

'Hi Eva,' he said. 'Um, nice to meet you.' His voice cracked sharply upwards and the women laughed in a way he would normally have found infuriating. Now, he was just glad for the voices.

Carol smiled. He could see the strain in her face now, and understood what all the unexplained staring at the funeral had been about, and why almost the entire town had turned up to the funeral of a man most people detested. 'Any family resemblance, you think?' she said.

Sam assessed Eva's face seriously. Her eyes were friendly and encouraging.

'You both have—' He looked from mother to daughter. '—the same mouth and maybe … maybe the same eyelashes?' The women laughed and it was the sound of flight, like the rush of air from a balloon.

'That's exactly what Helen and Elizabeth said!' exclaimed Eva. She pushed her fringe sideways across her forehead with the back of one hand. 'It's really great to meet you, Sam. I don't know if you know …' Here she looked to the older women for approval and their eyes and the tilt of their chins encouraged her. 'Once I found out Carol was my mother, I initially found her on Facebook and sent her a message. Very modern of me, hey? Not bad for a digital immigrant of 33.'

She smiled, and Sam grinned back. 'I hope you liked a few of her statuses first, before the message,' he said. 'Or at least "Eva became a fan of something that Carol is a fan of".'

Elizabeth raised her eyebrows. 'This is Elvish, what they're saying, isn't it?'

Helen shook her head. 'Wrong era, Queenie. Just pretend you understand but make sure you don't use the word "cool".' She paused. 'Or "techno". Or "cyber-anything".'

Sam grimaced. Helen pointed at him. 'See?'

The women laughed, and Sam marvelled at the difference between this group and the group he had stood in just minutes before. There'd been so much competition between the men. Even the ones who didn't know each other. Every sentence doubled as a challenge but every sentence among these women doubled as—he frowned, tried to place it. Every sentence here doubled as love.

A comfortable silence draped over the group. As usual, it was Helen who spoke first. 'Caro? You think it's about right now? They're probably too pissed to argue.'

Elizabeth nodded. 'I reckon,' she said loudly.

Carol bit her lip. Eva hesitated, then slid an arm around her mother's waist.

Carol curled hers around Eva's shoulders. They were almost exactly the same height.

Sam looked from woman to woman. Helen leaned towards him. 'Caro's going to say some things she wasn't allowed to say at the funeral,' she murmured, 'and we're going to shout down any of the boys who try to shut her up. You don't need to do anything, Sam. Don't be scared either, I don't think it's going to be a big deal. Stick close to me, sweetheart.'

Carol picked up a knife and dinged it against her teacup. It was such a small noise but it cut through the room like a swear word at a kitchen tea. Some neural pathway was triggered; even the loudest old men fell silent across their bellies.

'It's been a lovely day for Dad,' she began. Her words were careful. 'He would have been pleased with the turnout, and the ceremony was just what he would have wanted.'

A movement across the room caught Sam's eye: Des had stepped forward. But a man Sam didn't know caught Des's elbow, leaned forward and muttered something into his ear. There were just so many people Sam didn't know. Des pressed his lips together and stood still.

'You've probably all heard that Eva, my daughter,' Carol gestured, and Eva smiled confidently at the room, 'is here for this special occasion. I'd just like to welcome her to the family, even if it's a bit late. She's a smart, smart woman and she's got a fair bit of fight in her — Dad would have really liked that. He would have really liked her. It's a shame he couldn't have met her, but that's how it goes I guess. I guess you'll all agree that family is very important. I hope you'll welcome Eva to our family. Everyone says you can't choose your family, which is pretty right I think. Sometimes you can find your family, though. I don't know if that makes sense. You can't choose them, but you can find them. I'm very glad to have found Eva. Anyway, that's all I had to say. Get onto the sandwiches, boys, they're running low.'

The men rumbled off in groups. The kids resumed their shrieking conga lines and the elderly asked each other what Carol had said.

Sam raised his eyes as Eva, Elizabeth and his aunts curled in as a group. For a few moments it was just him and the four women. Then like an unexpected breaker, women from all over the room suddenly swept towards them. Some brought platters, some didn't. Everyone smelled like tea. A whirlpool of women circled the sisters and daughters — and Sam, the son. Warm, muscled arms blocked out the beefy gestures of the men. Floral and dark dresses completed the colour wheel; there were warm eyes and gentle hands on shoulders.

Helen spoke first. 'We're not glad of death,' she said firmly. 'Death is never a good thing. But we're glad to welcome new family today. Eva? Carol? We're glad for this. It's so good.'

Sam's hands hung by his sides. Among all these women he felt like a strange new incarnation, a new generation. He bit his lip, stared at the floor. On both sides, a warm hand clasped his own. Finally, he raised his head and saw the eyes of the women were as bright as his.

Oral sex
Judith A Green

'and then she said'
prayer-shaped human contours
stacked on seats in single layers or
hanging from overhead straps
sway with the motion of the metal beast
paying homage to a handheld device
as some find solace in rosary beads,
although their devotion is to a different god
'and then she said'
peals of laughter erupt, ricocheting between the contours
the ambience of the carriage jostled like a summer whirlwind
the motion of the beast undisturbed,
fingers momentarily stilled
'and then she said'
high-pitched words run races with laughter
tripping over uncontrolled giggles
anticipation swelling as an ocean swells before
crashing onto the sand
'and then she said,
what's oral sex?'
raucous laughter bounces off windows
stretching from floor to ceiling
girlish, out-of-control mirth filling the air space,
gasping,
'what did you say?'
the metal beast shudders to a breathless halt …
laughter tumbles out the door
rolling along the platform

Kurraga Bay
Primary School Carnival
Les Wicks

Come the day we make nothing in Australia
except a few new minds.
Queue them up, shhh
those tiny riots   be quiet
they dance under a corrosive loudspeaker
in a swish of corralled delight.
Music is scrubbed raw.
this primary school penitentiary with
its locked up nobles … their sceptres of bananas,
the ruby glow of Roll-Ups. These
are treasured prisoners.
Our future
already has its madnesses and monsters but
we look instead to the lightvoice, that insight
flowers on macadam, ignore
scraped knee betrayal as you write your mitigations, heavily lean on
best I could do under the circumstances, though we all will be
the guilty ones at the end.
The child in turn becomes the jailer
and the future is
our pen. Lives are an emergency,
hope for an attendance. This world
is dirty, hope for sprucing. We have given them
so many things they
will pay the bill someday. Our children
are just perfect (maybe perfectly just).
We hope for the former against all reason.

Cold currents
Susi Fox

His body is beige, the colour of silty mud. It only covers half the length of the ambulance stretcher.

I leap into action, attaching the line of pre-warmed fluid to the IV in the crook of the boy's arm, hooking up the hospital monitor with sticky purple circles on his pale chest, injecting adrenaline into his collapsed veins. I check the boy's temperature: thirty-four degrees.

The ambos' eyes are on me.

Trace, her belly pressed hard up against the trolley, has stopped squeezing the resuscitation bag like it's the boy's heart between her hands. The bag hangs slack in front of her.

Mick raises his eyebrows, his palms thumping the boy's chest. 'He's been down an hour already,' he says, one hand flicking greasy hair across his forehead, out of his eyes. 'In the water for at least fifteen before they found him.'

'You can call it now,' Trace says. One edge of the mask she's holding against the boy's face lifts from his cheek to reveal his violet lips beneath.

'Family wanted us to bring him in,' Mick says, 'but it's really just a formality, eh?' His compressions are so half-hearted, he seems to be massaging the boy's chest, rather than pumping it.

The stiffly-pressed sheet lining the stretcher is whiter than the boy's skin. It's the same type of sheet my son Jason used to complain was too scratchy, the odd nights he spent away from his mother's house on the floor of my spare room.

I suck another vial of adrenaline into the syringe, flick the air from the tip. 'Keep going,' I say. 'There's still a chance.'

Trace sighs beside me and squeezes the bag with renewed vigour, like perhaps someone's life depends on it after all. Mick resumes the chest compressions, his eyes downcast as he counts the beats.

The boy's lying still. His bare chest streaked with rivulets of muddy water streaming down either side of his torso, onto the white cotton beneath him, like the tears that swum across Jason's dusty cheeks when his mother told him she was moving back to the big smoke.

From the head of the bed, I bark instructions at the hospital nurses. Before they place the air warmer over him, I grab the scissors and cut into his sodden shorts. Denim, stretching down to his knees, flecked with dirt. I peel the shorts from his skin, scrunch them into a ball and place them under the trolley.

The last time I swam at the lake would have been over ten years ago now, with Jason by my side. He wouldn't have been much older than this boy. As we freestyled together back to shore, cold water eddies began to encircle my chest.

I couldn't breathe. I'd heard the rumours, that the cold currents from old mine shafts in the depths of the lake dragged people under the water, drowning them. I felt the undertow tugging on my ankles, enticing me down into the deep. I struggled, kicked my legs against the iciness, gulped the hot afternoon air into my lungs and, spluttering and heaving, paddled back through the dusky water to the shallows. Thank God Jason was already there, waiting for me.

'I thought you were gone, Dad,' he said.

So did I.

'He's gone, Dan,' Mick says. He flicks his hair behind his ear, avoiding my eyes, then removes his hands from the boy's chest and puts one palm on the sheet, like he's claiming him. 'Too late.'

'Keep going. We can bring him back.'

'He was stiff when we pulled him up. White, not blue.'

The heart monitor shows a flat line. The boy's lips are bluey purple, not a hint of red. The hospital nurses have all stepped back against the walls. Not one of them will meet my eyes.

'Keep going,' I say.

I draw up more adrenaline as the warm air almost floats over the boy's torso. My fingers fumble on his neck, feeling for a pulse.

'Only seven.' Drops of sweat flick from Mick's forehead onto the boy's damp curls. 'Went in after a ball.' The lake water has dripped across the boy's head and down his neck; the sheet under him is soaked.

'His parents will be here any minute,' Trace says, pressing her belly in harder to the trolley.

The scene to come shimmers to life in front of me. The young boy's mother will fall to her knees, shrieking. His father will stand with his back against the flimsy curtain as if it could hold him up. I'll back slowly from the cubicle, clutching the notes, trying to avoid eye contact, wondering what they regret about their family life, and about themselves.

My hand is clutching the boy's clammy wrist. I place the syringe into the IV in his arm and I'm just about to push the plunger when I catch sight of his eyes, open wide and staring. Despite the glare of the overhead lights, his irises seem to have a matt coating, like greasy wax. He's not looking at me, or Mick, or Trace. He's not looking at anything at all.

I place the syringe down on the resuscitation cart and step back from the trolley. I cross my arms across my chest.

'Stand down,' I say to the nurses clustered around the edges of the room. 'You can pack everything away.'

Mick is already starting to pull a sheet up over the body. There's a smudge of dirt on one of the boy's cheeks. I go to wipe it off but Mick grabs my wrist before I can touch his pale skin. 'Coroner's, Dan.'

I stretch the sheet slowly over the dead kid's face, smoothing out the edges of the sheet so there are no wrinkles. I can still see his dark ringlets where the sheet doesn't quite meet the pillow.

Mick flicks the metal rails of the trolley with his index finger. 'Up for a drink tonight? Trace and I thought we might head to the Royal with a couple of the SES guys.'

'Maybe next time, eh?' I take the paperwork he's handing to me across the body. Time for the formalities.

Up close to the body, there's a faint odour of mud floating in the air, like mould. I bring my wrist to my nose, covering my nostrils. Even with the bulbs of the stethoscope plugging my ears, I can still hear the ambos catching up on local gossip with the nursing staff. I think I catch a brief *luddup* in the stethoscope diaphragm and I almost cry out. I keep listening, straining to hear even the faintest pinpoint of a pulse. Nothing. The *luddup* must have been my own blood squealing through the arteries deep in my inner ears. When I ease the stethoscope out from under the sheet, it flicks the boy's hand so it dangles down towards the ground. I replace his hand beside him on the trolley and tuck the sheet in under it.

'… mother and brother will be up soon. Pretty upset. Family holiday. Went in after a ball,' Mick's saying to the nurses, in case they hadn't caught it the first time, his hands unplugging leads from the monitors with only the slightest tremble.

I pick up the ED phone and dial the Coroner's Court. As the phone rings and rings, the dead boy's eyes float into my vision, large and inky as they stare up at the ceiling. They're the same as Jason's used to look, when I'd creep into his room after late nights on-call. I would pull his eyelids down gently over his dilated pupils, seat myself on the end of his bed and watch him breathe.

Jason doesn't remember me closing his eyes like that in the middle of the night. He told me once that he still sleeps with his eyes open, that it doesn't bother his girlfriend at all. I stay silent when the two of them visit, his feet up on my coffee table, her dark curls cascading down over the back of my sofa. It's been quite a while since they last came to stay.

The dead kid's parents will be here before too long. I hang up and dial Jason's number. He picks up on the seventh ring.

'It's your dad,' I say. 'Me.'

'Yes, Dad. You're the only person who calls the home phone now. Gemma and I are getting rid of it next month. Too expensive.'

I lower my head to sniff myself. The smell of the lake seems to have penetrated my clothes: the dampness of lake creatures, tiny micro-organisms in a pool of murky water. 'You coming to visit any time soon?'

'Yes, Dad.' He coughs, his hand covering the speaker. 'But we're so busy. So much going on up here. You should move to the city, you know.'

He says it every time I call. He hasn't seen the teetering towers of paperwork on my desk, the unread medical journals, the relentless case notes I haven't had a chance to finish.

I close my eyes. The words are out before I can stop them: 'Maybe I'll come for a visit. Next week, perhaps.'

'Yes, Dad.' His voice is nonchalant; he's playing with Gemma's hair, or just watching TV.

I clear my voice and pause. 'Jason,' I say, although I know what he'll say, I just want to hear him say it, a boyish lilt in his voice as he chimes, *Yes, Dad*, the same every time I call. 'Jason, do you still sleep with your eyes open?'

The volta
Siobhan Hodge

Thirteen again, watching
the dust settle. A rangy grey
has stepped out of line,
drawn thin
in sand so soft
it may not
have stirred at all.
I remember no slight,
no move that could
have provoked your ire.
Primed between line and rod,
I am only dull witness
to your assault.
The rope is chucked, hiss
belly-deep.
Hooves spin
spent circles.
A half-moon gaze
that cannot lift higher.
Wilted mane
too long to braid
gummed down
with sweat and silt.
His fearful pace
stirs and
your crop, antenna in electrical
storm, is now a coiled snake,
squat and spoiling.
Just try it, mate.
The children watched
your shoulders slick back, rigid
certainty. *Show him who's boss*
or some such epithet, ink watered
by time, but I have seen your legacy
clutching spurs with more tenderness

than mane.
I see him still,
that lean body
lacquered with sweat.
The whip in your hand
wasn't needed; your face alone
struck him down, each trembling
ear swivelled for contact.
Not this battery of energy,
crackling and shorting out,
pinioned between shed wall
and eye that would not yield
even the smallest ground
for error.
That line may sink, unstrung,
last lesson unlearned
among the hills and hands.
For now, I will no more
codify your violence
than that damned horse could.

Homeless

Mark William Jackson

I am a thing / not a thing
elevated to the status
of object / product
a float between what
you've seen / thought you saw
                / ignored
the error of our ways
is the tragedy of our days
how long until O becomes Q
until the realisation gains a tail
and the question of de-evolution
is reconsidered by apes
on a production line
look, squatted in a shopfront
under discoloured blankets
the disgrace of our lives
thrown from the line
I am a thing / not a thing

The black flower

Kristian Guagliardo

Have you ever noticed the car parked out the front of the bottlo at eight-thirty in the morning?

That's not a rhetorical question: I'm actually asking, because it's the reason I used to drive five kilometres out of my way to the Irish-themed bottlo to get my morning bourbon.

If I'd gone to my local bottlo, that would've been the moment, I had thought, when my boss would've driven past and raised an eyebrow. Or Dad would just happen to have been driving past and would've called me and to ask what I was doing and I would've told a stupid lie like 'still in bed' or 'at work, Dad' while he could clearly see me warming my hands with my breath outside the closed roller shutters.

But that was before. Nowadays I don't give a shit.

I've refined my mornings down to a syncopated rhythm. My housemate Nick is a labourer and he's outta the house by about six at the latest. I know when he's up 'cause his alarm is Acca Dacca and if there's one thing that can wake you from a drunken stupor, it's 'Highway to Hell'.

I wait until the door clicks shut and I can hear his boots crunching away on the metal dust and then I'm up. Blinking, bleary, crook in the guts. But already something unmistakeable is happening in the pit of my stomach: excitement.

Excitement doesn't quite cut it, but I can't explain it much better. Even on mornings when the sun coming through the venetians pierces my eyes and my head is thumping like a wacker packer, I start thinking about that first sip and it starts to grow like a flower in my solar plexus. It gives me goosebumps. It's like being horny but even stronger. The more you think about it, the more you want it.

This morning I am awake before the riffs blare out of Nick's speakers. I'm champing at the bit by the time his boots crunch away. I chuck the sheets off and stumble straight to the kitchen. Nick and I are both single so the fridge is still unsullied by bossy girlfriends: it's ninety per cent VB, Emu and Swan, eight per cent steak and two per cent whatever's in that weird brown container on the top shelf.

Cold beer down my throat. I always scull the first one and feel the happy tingle in my stomach and the loving flush of my face.

Beer number two follows immediately. I have it on the back patio with a smoke. For me, it's the best part of the day: the sky still grey and pink, like a galah; the air crisp and cold; the smell of tobacco smoke mixed with grog. I hunch over the table and check the footy forums on my phone for the latest. There's nothing new.

'Robbo.'

The voice electrocutes my nerves. Nick is standing at the door of the patio.

'Thought you left,' I say.

'Forgot these,' Nick says, pair of white PPE gloves in his hand. 'You just get home or what?'

'Nah, wasn't out.'

'You were home last night? I thought you were out.'

'Nah, was just in my room, man.' Nursing a bottle of Wild Turkey before I passed out.

Nick looks at the nearly-empty stubby next to my phone. He looks upset for some reason. 'You got work today, don't ya, Robb?'

'Yeah, nah, startin' at twelve today, man,' I lie, not looking him in the eyes. I don't think he's buying it any more. What kind of mechanic starts work at noon? 'S'all good, I got time for a coupla cold ones.'

Nick shakes his head. 'Mad dog,' he mutters. But it's different to how he used to call me 'mad dog' a week or two ago. I didn't know until now that there were two ways of saying that.

He jerks his head up by way of leave-taking and slides the patio door shut.

I take a deep drag on my cigarette. Might be time to move on from Nick's. He used to be a mad cunt, Jägerbombs all the time and absinthe and Flaming Sambucas. Now he's starting to lose his edge, just like every housemate I've had over the last few months. They start out acting like a party animal, like me, but it only lasts a week or two. Next thing ya know, they or their fucken bossy girlfriends tell me I'm a bad influence and I need to go.

Beers three, four and five go down in front of the Xbox. I'm better at *Call of Duty* when I've had a few to take the edge off. I lose track of time sitting on the beanbag with my arse going numb.

I usually have my sixth beer in the shower. There's nothing better sometimes than a shower beer. Makes getting ready for the day just that bit more bearable.

Six beers is enough of a start: time for something harder. I leave the house at eight. Pull my beanie on and jump in the old Nissan and fire her up. It takes two goes this morning. Piece of shit's on the way out.

On my way to the bottlo, a cop car pulls up next to me at a set of lights.

'Fuck!' I say, forgetting my window is down.

The cop riding shotgun looks around: he's a blond bloke and looks like a dead-set tosser. I feel my eyes getting sucked towards his and accidentally catch his gaze briefly before looking forward, gripping the steering wheel with two hands. I don't think I had two hands on it before. I stare at the traffic ahead of me and feel the cop's eyes burning on my cheek. Time passes like molasses. Then the light goes green and the cops zoom forward and I quickly chuck a left to get the fuck away.

I get about a hundred metres down the road and just start cracking up. They had no idea. And I've never seen anyone get breathalysed at eight am on a bloody Tuesday morning.

I have to dog-leg through some back streets to get back on course but I still rock up at the local shopping centre before the bottlo opens. The car park is devoid of human life: a few parked cars, weedy potholes in the old bitumen and a big sign with half the letters missing so it says 'Wood Pla' instead of 'Woodvale Plaza'. I turn the ignition off, rubbing my hands together to warm them before lighting a smoke. And now I wait.

Just after twenty past, a blonde woman pulls up in a battered white Barina beside me. Her hair is a bird's nest and she's got no makeup on. She shoulders a nappy bag while trying to get her whinging baby out of the back.

I roll the window down. 'You need a hand?'

The woman jumps about ten feet into the air, glances around like a twitching mouse, then goes back to unstrapping her baby.

'I can hold your bag if you need,' I offer again. 'Or your baby. I'm great with kids. I can make 'em laugh real easy.'

This time she doesn't even turn around. She scoops her baby up with one arm, not even supporting the head properly, and scampers away across the carpark.

'Fucken rude bitch!' I yell out. 'Just tryin'a help!'

I get out of my car and light up another durry, but it doesn't even take the edge off. Sometimes a smoke isn't good for anything. I wish I'd had a seventh beer and just left home later. I hate having to wait for booze.

I pace back and forth in front of the bottlo. My head is thumping again. My hands are trembling. I look at my phone. Eight-thirty! Why aren't the shutters up? I knock on the shutter three times; the whole thing reverberates metallically and I wait, but nothing happens.

'Come *on*!' I shout through the shutter. 'Get your fucken acts together!'

Another five or ten minutes pass and there's no action. I bang on the shutters a few more times but nobody opens up. For fuck's sake.

I turn away from the shutters to light another smoke and I freeze in my tracks. The cops from the traffic lights have just pulled into the car park.

I freeze and lean against the shutters of the bottlo, scrolling through my phone as casually as I can, glancing up every few seconds to track the paddy wagon. It creeps along the perimeter of the car park, way beyond the main shopping centre entrance, before pulling up right next to me.

The cops get out. The blond tosser is a beefy bloke and looks real dirty on me. The driver is a woman cop, a brunette. She actually has a killer rack, but all caged up in that blue police uniform it's a bit of a turn-off.

I look down at my phone and try to pretend they aren't there. At least I'm not driving.

The cops start to move, jangling loudly with their chains or keys or whatever they have on them that makes that noise. The noise stops about three feet away from me. The sun is suddenly out of my eyes.

The bloke clears his throat and I look up. 'Can I help you, officers?'

'G'day mate, I'm Constable Adam White and this is my colleague, Constable Nadine Pleet. We've received a complaint from the staff here about a disturbance this morning. D'you know anything about that?'

'Nah, I haven't seen nothin'. They haven't even opened yet and it's quarter to nine.'

'This store opens at nine am,' says Constable Pleet.

'No kidding?' I say, looking at the little red sign beside the shutter. Son of a bitch. She's right.

'The store manager reported someone pounding on the door and yelling abuse at staff,' Constable White says. He crosses his arms. 'I think that mighta been you, mate.'

'Nah.' I shrug. 'I did knock on the shutters, but that's it, you know. Just tryin'a get a pressie for me dad's birthday, it's today. He likes bourbon.'

'Our report was that you threatened to smash these shutters in,' Constable White says.

'Piss off!' I cry. 'You can't just put words in my mouth, jeez! I told you it wasn't me!'

'A tattooed male youth wearing ripped jeans, a red ice hockey jersey and a beanie. Are you saying there're two of you around this morning, mate?' Constable Pleet says. 'We need you to move along.'

'This is fucked!' I spit. 'You cops are always pickin' on me, I didn't do nothin'.'

'Move along,' White says.

'Fucken hell,' I say, moving for my car. 'Well, thanks a lot, my old man's not gonna get a birthday present thanks to youse, happy now?'

'Keep moving,' White says, like a real wanker.

'Fucken dumb cunts,' I mutter loud enough for them to hear.

I get about two metres from my car when I realise I can't get behind the wheel or they'll do me for drink-driving. I change course and head for the shopping centre entrance. I look back over my shoulder and the cops are both still standing guard out the front of the bottlo, arms crossed like complete tossers. I pull the finger and I know they see it, but they don't move.

'Fucken poxy shithole,' I curse as I walk into the shops. I figure I'll kill some time here 'til the cops piss off, then go back and get my bourbon.

I pace around, looking at the shops. It's all shit and old and decaying. Half the lights don't work.

'You want come in?'

I turn around to see a little Chinese woman. She's in a red and white polo shirt and, as with most Asian women, I can't be sure if she's thirty or sixty.

'What?'

'You want massage? Only thirty-five dollar today, on special.'

I stare at her for about twenty seconds before realising that I've been standing in front of a tiny massage parlour. Huh. Maybe a rub 'n' tug would do me good until the cops bugger off.

'Okay,' I say.

She waves me into the parlour. Panpipe music is playing. The air smells both sweet and savoury. The masseuse beckons me into a curtained-off cubicle with a long wooden table. She puts a wicker basket on the table.

'Clothes in here. Keep pants on. Okay?' She draws the curtain.

Keep pants on – sure, lady. I strip down to my jocks and lay face down.

A little voice says, 'Okay, you ready?'

'Mm hmm,' I mutter.

She enters. 'No, no, pants on!' she chides. She covers my arse with a towel and begins squirting cold oil on my back. Her hands glide over my back muscles, thumbs crunching the knots in my back with the force of a man.

I suddenly realise, with a surge of disappointment, that this is a legit massage joint. I'm not gonna be copping a hand job today. There's a checkout scanner bleeping in the background from the supermarket. The customers who come in after me are mother and daughter. Someone in the back of the parlour is trying to get a baby to sleep.

'My new grandson,' the Chinese masseuse apologises, then adds something in angry Mandarin to someone on the other side of the curtain. The baby's crying disappears out a back door. 'Two week old.'

'Congrats,' I say. Six beers is nowhere near enough to wreck me, but it does loosen my tongue enough for me to blurt out, 'You're lucky. I was gonna have a son a few months ago.'

'Ah, you have baby boy, too? But you so young!'

'Nah – I was goin' to, but …' The words die in my throat as the lump swells.

'How old your son?' the masseuse asks. We aren't having the same conversation.

'Uh … he'd'a bin … a week old by now.'

'Oh, so nice! He look like you?'

'Uh huh,' I choke.

'What his name?'

'Um. Daniel. I wanted to call him Daniel.'

I feel the tingle in my gut again, the urge to obliterate stronger than ever. I close my eyes but all I can think of is my son who never was, the only flicker of light I had before he got snuffed out. I don't know how it really happened but I always imagine him swimming around in the womb, such a happy little dude, and then the drugs kicking in and his little heart stopping and him floating to the top of the amniotic sac, like a dead fish.

I never saw his mother again. She moved house, then broke the news about the baby in a text. 'Got rid of it yesterday. Couldn't have a kid by myself and I'm NOT gonna raise a kid around a drunk deadbeat FUCK like you if you WON'T STOP DRINKIN!!!'

I'd called her twenty times with no answer. She texted back, 'YOU made this happen, Robb, NOT ME!!'

The masseuse works some magic on me. I fall asleep at some point; I only know this because I suddenly awaken to a sharp smack on my head.

'Ouch! What the fuck?'

'Out – you go, get out now!' the Chinese lady squawks.

I get up, confused. An odour catches my nostrils. It smells like the massage oil went rancid. It's not until I feel the warm moisture in my jocks that I understand.

'Naughty boy – out, go!' the masseuse cries.

I don't say anything. I throw my jeans on, forgetting my shirt, and walk out of the massage parlour numbly, piss trickling down my legs. Not my fault. Coulda happened to anyone.

I walk into the carpark. The cops are gone. I gravitate to the open bottlo and buy a bottle of cheap bourbon. I get back into the Nissan but my gut is already tingling in anticipation. The black flower blossoms in my chest. No time to go home. Shirtless and sodden, I twist the cap off the bottle, slide the brown paper down, lock my quivering lips around the warm glass neck and drink until I am empty.

Roof tiles
Laura Brinson

From the bus window
terracotta roofs gently undulate
waves of half-pipe tiles
baked earth in russet tones
on listing framework
brick-red or darkened with age
drooping with leaf litter
blackened with lichen
crumbling piles gather
under the eaves
timber slumps
corners sag
tiles chip and loosen
the centre bows and smiles
a gap-toothed grin

The magnolia tree
Kristen Roberts

Arlie raises the blind to find Codger shaking the magnolia tree. Leaves litter the grass at his feet, their celebration of the waning heat cut short by his single-minded pursuit of order. He mutters as he grasps each branch, agitating loose the leaves that will fly and plucking free those that won't. The rake and bin wait like deputies by the fence.

Codger loves this tree. Its limbs, gnarled and stout, are pruned of unnecessary offshoots. He maintains a meticulous circle of rich earth around its base, tending regularly both to the border and the bulbs that hibernate beneath the surface. He waters it judiciously in summer, when the tree's hand-sized leaves provide glorious shade for the rear of the house, and feeds it a complex range of nutrients in early spring when it produces large, velveteen blooms, the purple of which complements the irises that emerge below. The magnolia flowers remind Arlie of vaginas. They look, to her, like proud vulvas exposing their secrets to the sky. Codger was indignant when she'd told him, suggesting that perhaps she'd watched too many late night programs on SBS before busying himself with the jammed latch on the laundry window. She'd spied him later that afternoon though, a magnolia flower cupped in one rough hand and a quizzical smile on his face. Now that it's autumn, however, the tree drives him mad. Every day he rakes beneath it, and each morning he finds that the front-line of the autumnal army has advanced again.

Today, apparently, he has decided to take control of the situation. Arlie takes a mint from her pocket and a pencil from the jar on her desk. She narrows her eyes at Codger, too engrossed in the tree to have yet noticed her, and begins to sketch him. The mint rattles against the cage of her teeth as the charcoal captures the tense line of his jaw.

He wasn't always known as Codger. Arlie fell in love with John, the no-nonsense man with the no-nonsense name, who was raised on the post-war foundations of pride, respect and honesty. Sometimes gruff and usually quiet, he was a good man, and Arlie had known he would always take care of her and their children. She knows that women look for more than that now, for men who use facial products and carry their babies about in slings and discuss their feelings. Men more adept in the construction of arancini balls than garden sheds; but that kind of man hadn't existed back then. She's not sure what she'd do if Codger did anything more towards preparing dinner than getting out the salt mill and tomato sauce.

What she does know, however, is that somewhere along the way his disdain for newspaper-boys who couldn't throw clear onto the front porch had metastasised. He had begun grumbling about drivers who didn't indicate for long enough before turning and people who lined up in the express lane of the supermarket with more than eight items, and then teenagers who wore their pants too low ('so far down their backsides you can see their breakfast!'), and the short life-expectancy of modern electronics and the sensationalisation of news by the media. In short, he had become crotchety. Always a stickler for the rules, he had officially become a grumpy old man before he was even truly old. Mid-career, the younger crew on the ship had taken to calling him 'the grumpy old codger', and when his peers caught wind of the nickname it had stuck. Now, when he cuts the camellias from the tree as they bloom purely so that they won't have the chance to brown in the rain, she can hardly remember ever calling him John.

Arlie replicates the detail of the tree with a practised economy and shades the undersides of the branches, craggy and vulnerable in their new exposure. She has drawn this tree many times over the years, usually when stuck for ideas but unwilling to stop making lines on the page. Codger is now raking. This, too, is familiar territory. There is something in his stance, in the flex of his body ushering the leaves towards the bin and the lawn towards bareness; he is comfortable now, with order almost within reach. Arlie pushes the drawing aside and reaches instead for the proofs of her latest illustrations. They look good – she's pleased with the colour saturation but wonders if there should be an extra rabbit on page three. She pencils it in but finds that her heart isn't really in it, so returns to the picture of her husband and the magnolia tree instead.

The lawn now immaculate, Codger has the rake wrong way up and is swiping at the stubborn leaves at the top of the tree. Arlie ignores him emphatically and deepens the contrast of her branches, enhancing the light that thatches the upper canopy. Then Codger swears, loudly enough that the swooping vowels of his words thud against the windowpane – the rake is stuck, and his attempts to free it are far from balletic. Arlie snorts, and Codger steps away from the tree. Hands on hips, he gazes up to the sky and then at the ground as if searching for some greater understanding, and finally notices his wife. He gestures at the rake and shrugs and then, with a wry smile and a wink, stalks off towards the shed. Arlie smiles quietly to herself. Her pressure on the pencil imperceptibly firmer than before, she plays again with the lines of the magnolia tree and draws a fatal flaw though its trunk.

Macalister
Paul Mill

I t is still raining when she gets out of bed in the morning. In the kitchen her dad is on the phone. His shoulders are bunched up around his ears from the cold, and he's wearing that oversized wool jumper that Mum knitted for him, its cuffs starting to fray where he's rolled up the sleeves. He nods thoughtfully, with that look on his face he has when he is concentrating on not correcting someone. A cup of tea sits on the windowsill in front of him, tendrils of steam rising off it. She could hear him during the night, after the storm came in, shuffling around the house like an old dog that can't find a comfortable place to sleep.

'Best not to come and pick her up, road's probably out,' he says. 'You don't want to get stuck further down in the valley.' He shifts his weight from one foot to the other. 'No, we're okay. I'll call the school to let them know that she won't be in today.' He brings the cup of tea to his mouth and sips carefully at it. 'She can afford to miss a day of school.'

He looks at her and murmurs, 'Morning,' an odd grin on his face that she doesn't understand. 'I've got to go,' he says to the phone. 'No, everything's orright.'

He breathes out through his nose, mouth tightly closed like it's been sewn shut.

He tells the girl, 'No point opening the shop today. Don't think I'll be able to get you to school either.'

'I heard.'

'Little pitchers have big ears.'

She stands next to her dad, waiting for him to put his arm across her shoulders. He shifts his weight to the other leg, and then extends an arm around her shoulders to bring her towards him. He's warm, like he's carrying a fever. She feels him breathe in and hold his breath. Now that she's out of bed her feet are itchy from the cold air coming up through the floorboards.

'I'll light a fire,' he tells her. 'Don't want you to get sick.'

She shivers, wraps her arms around his waist. 'I'm okay,' she says. She thinks she should be too old for this. She thinks, *bet the other girls at school aren't like this with their dads.*

'Still,' he says. He's looking out at the carpark for the shop. It's under a couple of inches of water and the only vehicle out there is Macalister's van, tucked underneath the branches of one of the ghost gums. She looks past her father at the logo on the side of Macalister's van: *R&M Hiking Tours.*

Her father has told her, *watch out for Macalister, don't trust him for a second.* She watches Macalister through the windows of their shop when he brings a group of hikers in his tour bus. The hikers come into the shop smelling of camphor and stale dirt; they buy bottles of water and energy bars and shoelaces and garbage bags to keep things dry when it looks like it might rain, but Macalister stays out by the van, leaning against its side door. He'll roll a cigarette, the packet of loose leaf tobacco tucked between his elbow and his ribs, then bring it to his mouth and light it with a Bic that he's produced from the chest pocket of his waterproof jacket.

'Last minute supplies,' he'll tell them. 'The bastard won't gouge you. At least, not too much.' He says this with a smile on his face, revealing crooked yellow teeth.

She wants to bring a hand up to her mouth when she sees him, so she won't reveal the braces that she has to correct her own crooked teeth.

Her dad steps away, taking his warmth with him. The window frames on one side of the house rattle from a gust of wind. 'Power might go out soon,' he tells her as he scans the sky through the window, eyebrows furrowed. 'Best be prepared for that.'

***

Later in the morning she hears the sound of boots on the wooden slats of the verandah. She looks at her father, sees his face change when he hears them too.

'What bloody fool—' he starts to say, but he is interrupted by someone knocking on the door.

A voice calls out her dad's name. 'Jake, you home?'

It's odd to hear anyone calling her dad by his first name; usually it's just the two of them and she doesn't think of him having an identity other than Dad.

The voice calls out, 'Jake, it's Macalister, you home?'

Her dad shivers as he walks to the door. He pulls down the sleeves of his oversized jumper so that they cover his hands. Without shoes on, he walks on the outside of his feet, bandy-legged, like he's in one of those old cowboy movies.

'Not inside,' her dad says at the door. Macalister steps back. Over his shoulders hangs a backpack. Little puddles of water are forming at his feet. Her dad closes the door behind him.

She hears murmuring voices. She hears her dad say, 'You look like a drowned rat.' She strains her ears to try to hear more. She is waiting for her father to get angry, the anticipation like the barometric pressure dropping just before a summer storm.

The phone rings. Her dad calls out, 'Tammy, can you get that?'

It's her grandmother. Her mum's mum. She asks the girl if she can speak to her dad, to make sure that everything is still all right.

'He can't come to the phone,' she says. 'He just stepped away for a moment.'

She doesn't want to tell her grandmother about Macalister. She's seen the photos, that old album full of pictures of them at parties and Christmas lunches and on holiday, pictures of her mum and him. Macalister not afraid of showing off his crooked teeth, smiling as her mum kisses him on the cheek. Pictures of them in a pub somewhere, performing on a small stage in the corner, her mum singing with her eyes closed, Macalister playing an acoustic guitar while he looks at her.

'I just want to make sure that everything is all right,' her grandmother replies.

'Everything is okay,' she says.

'I miss you.'

The girl knows what's coming next.

But first she hears her father say, 'Okay, we'll do that,' and she is startled by the door opening again, the chill from the air outside and the sound of the rain. She looks up to see Macalister looking in, hands stuffed into the pockets of his Gore-Tex jacket. The glimpse is only for a moment before her father closes the door again.

'You know, you could stay with us more if you wanted to,' her grandmother tells her. 'Would be easier for your father, he wouldn't need to drive you to school during the week.' She pauses for a moment, and the girl takes a breath in. 'And a girl your age should be closer to her friends,' her grandmother says.

But she's not really listening.

'My boots,' he starts to ask her, 'where are my hiking boots?' He sees them just as he says the end of the sentence. He walks over the fireplace and lets out a moan when he bends down to pick them up.

'I have to go now,' she tells her grandmother. 'Dad needs me.'

As she hangs up the phone, she hears him say, 'Bloody Macalister,' in a quiet voice.

He sniffs twice, rubs at an eyebrow with his dirty fingers. He looks like he is about to say something, then stops. 'I've got to go out for a little while,' he says. 'When you hear us come back, I want you to stay here until I say it's okay. I don't want you sticking that beak of yours out the windows.'

'Dad, I—'

He cuts her short. 'Did you hear what I said?'

She nods.

'Let me hear you say it.'

'Stay here till you come back. Don't look outside the windows.'

He places a hand on her shoulders. 'Good girl,' he says. 'I won't be too long.'

There's a smell about him, wet dirt and wood chips. The fathers of the girls she goes to school with, they don't smell like that. They come to parent nights wearing suits and ties and polished leather shoes. Her dad, with that funk about him: t-shirts with the neck stretched out, cheap acrylic jumpers, trying to pretend for her sake that he doesn't feel out of place. He'll rest his hand on her shoulders and she'll feel herself tense up.

Teachers will come up to him. 'You must be Tammy's dad.'

He'll squeeze her shoulders at the sound of her name, like she's someone famous.

'Yup,' he'll say.

'Is your wife here too?'

She'll look up at him, say something like, *Dad, this is Mr Walsh, he teaches me English*. She'll place a hand on top of his hand to stop it sliding off her shoulder.

***

She stays in the armchair in front of the fire until she hears the sound of the shed door closing and then she counts to ten. She puts down her book and runs to the window, pressing her nose to the cold of the glass just in time to see Macalister leading her dad up the hiking trail behind the shop, up into the hills.

The two of them are carrying a stretcher. Once they are out of sight, she watches the rain fall, watches the little creeks of water run past the shop and into the carpark, all the way down to where Macalister has parked the van. She can still see on the side, written in carrot-orange paint, the words *R&M Hiking Tours*.

***

After she'd seen the photographs, she started to wonder how well Macalister knew her mum. She'd watch him on Sunday afternoon when he'd bring a group down the hill and into the valley. Same curly hair. Same stick-out ears. She'd realise that her hand was over her nose, thumb and forefinger on either side. Mum's button nose.

She remembers little things about her mum. The colour of her hair, the way her hands felt when she touched her, her smell in the mornings, the way she looked at her father, the way she said his name. Her mum was pretty, prettier than she'll ever be, no matter what her dad tells her. She had tiny shoulders and small boobs and a big bum. She tries to remember what it sounded like when she sang while she worked in the shop, how her voice echoed around the room and how people could hear it as they came past the shop on the way back down the hill. It's like something she can almost hear, but once she strains too hard it's gone, and then the only noise she can hear is the sound of her own heart beating.

***

Macalister and her dad come back down the hill a couple of hours later, her father leading the way. Their boots and pants are covered in red mud and Macalister's jacket is torn down the back, its two halves flapping in the wind. Between then they still carry the stretcher, but now there is a sleeping bag laid out on it, and when she looks at it a bit more she realises that there is something in the sleeping bag.

Then she realises what is in the sleeping bag.

Macalister seems careful, short words, sentences cut off halfway through. Saying more with his fingers than with his mouth. *A bit to the … yup, that's it … no more … perfect.*

They place the body on the floor of the van. When her father stands up, he reaches back with one hand to the base of his spine.

Through the windows of the van she can see her father offering his hand.

Macalister looks at it for a moment.

Her father says something to him, and then Macalister nods his head. He shakes her father's hand.

She watches as they close the sliding doors of the van behind them, and then, when they start to walk back to the house, she runs back to the armchair she had been sitting in when her father left. She hears the twin sets of footsteps scuffle on the wooden slats of the verandah, then murmured voices, the heel-toe pounding of her father's boots, the creak of the wooden chairs as he sits down on one of them, the low moan when he takes off his shoes.

She looks up when the door opens.

Her father says to her, 'Put the kettle on, would you Tammy?'

She looks closely at Macalister. Same curly hair and crooked teeth. Doesn't want to smile to show him her braces in case he gets mad. His face is dirty and he smells like a rainforest. Rough calloused hands like her father, but with nicotine stains between the joints of his fingers.

'Tammy,' her dad says, 'put the kettle on, would you?'

She nods, does as she is told.

From the kitchen, she hears Macalister say, 'It's odd how much she looks like Ruthie. Looks exactly like her at that age.'

***

Later that night her dad tells her, 'It's odd when you're not around. Quieter. Even at night when you're sleeping there's a noise about you that means I don't have to think.'

She looks at him.

'Oh, sweetie,' he tells her, 'it's just my way of telling you that I miss you when you're not here.'

'I know, Dad.'

He interrupts her. 'You know, I'm not good at saying these things, but I need to make sure that you know that.'

'I miss you too,' she says, but she's not sure how convincing it sounds.

'When you go to university you may only want to come back some weekends. Maybe live with some friends. And that's okay. I got plenty of stuff to keep me busy.'

She thinks of the things that he's taught her that the other girls at school don't know. What to do when someone gets bit by a snake, how to tie a bandage, how to fix a fence and how to warn people when it's too dangerous to go up the road that leads to the national park, and then shrug her shoulders when they don't listen. How to tie knots that don't slip. How to tell if someone's got heatstroke. What to tell the operator when you dial triple-zero. All the old dirt roads that they don't print on maps. Where the abandoned church is, with its cemetery out the back that smells of moss and weeds. How to light a fire. She bets the other girls at school don't know how to do that. She bets that most of their dads wouldn't be able to light a fire.

She thinks, I don't care about Macalister.

Beginning with a given line
Rodney Williams

After Naomi D.

taking a break from a paintbrush
having a rest from haiku
putting poetry
and prose
paragraphs
and parallels
on hold
finding a gap
between lines
formed by pen
and pencil
pastel
and print
to let the lungs
of my fancy
my love
for balance
between abstractions
my penchant
for distractions
within a moment
take a big deep breath
and sigh

Contributor Bios

Sarah Andrews is currently about to complete the last semester of BA/Creative Writing at RMIT. She is a mature-age student and single mother, currently committed to completing a memoir called *Home* about a tumultuous life and a person overcoming many adversities, finally choosing to write.

Laura Brinson has toured country festivals with one-act plays, dug for gold in Western Australia and walked the trail to Machu Picchu. She is a funeral celebrant and costume seamstress, currently living in Melbourne. Her prose and poetry has appeared in *Regime, Social Alternatives, n-Scribe* and *Mark My Words*.

Virginia Danahay is an archaeology and literature major who is currently at home excavating with her two-year-old son. Virginia has been published in *page seventeen* and *Pendulum*.

Liam Donnelly is a creative writing student from Geelong, currently studying at Deakin University.

Stefan Dubczuk is a Perth architect and Fellow of the Australian Institute of Architects. Awards include the Glen Phillips Poetry Prize 2013. Shortlisted: ACU 2015 Poetry Prize and SecondBite Poetry Competition 2014. Longlisted: Best Australian Poems 2014. Published: PCWC E-Magazine; 'Memory Weaving' and 'Peace, Tolerance & Understanding' anthologies.

Susi Fox is a GP in rural Victoria and is studying Professional Writing and Editing at RMIT. She is currently working on her first novel.

Judith A Green has played with words for many years with some success in competitions and being published. Her greatest joy, however, comes when words paint the images she carries deep within and a reader somewhere senses a connection.

Kristian Guagliardo is a Perth-based writer originally from Geraldton. He graduated from a Bachelor of Arts with Honours at Edith Cowan University in 2013. His creative writing has been published in *Indigo Journal* and in 2015 he received a highly-competitive ArtStart grant. He is currently completing a young adult novel.

Krystle Herdy is a Melbourne-based writer and poetry editor. Her first collection of poetry, *Mythology Mechanic*, was published in 2011.

Daniel Harper is a Melbourne-based writer with an interest in the intersection of travel writing and short fiction. This story was inspired by people he worked with in rural Africa and the BBC documentary 'Don't Panic – The Truth About Population'. Another of Dan's stories appears in *Sleepers Almanac X*. danharper321@gmail.com

Siobhan Hodge has a doctorate in English from the University of Western Australia, where she studied Sappho's poetry and translation. She has had poetry and criticism published in several places, including *Cordite, Limina, Plumwood Mountain, Kitaab,* and *Writ Review.* She also nurtures a passion for training horses.

Willa Hogarth's short stories have been published in *page seventeen, visible ink* and online with *Field of Words.* As a winner of the English 2011 Bluethumbnail Short Story Competition, she earned a writer's retreat in Greece and has garnered success in other competitions. She is currently working on a novella.

Mark William Jackson's work has appeared in various journals including *Best Australian Poems, Popshot, Going Down Swinging, Cordite, Rabbit Poetry Journal, Verity La* and *Tincture.* For more information visit markwmjackson.com.

Carmel Lillis is a secondary school teacher who lives in Melbourne's western suburbs with her husband and children. She is interested in writing short stories that explore social justice issues. Her work has been published in five editions of *Award Winning Australian Writing, Four W, Forty South* and *NSW School Magazine.*

Kerstin Lindros migrated to Australia in 1991. She studies Writing, History and Australian Studies at Deakin University. Her work has appeared in *Meanjin, Gangway, Sächsische Zeitung,* parenting magazines and Geelong Writers' anthologies. Kerstin writes in English and German to remain fluent in both languages as they evolve.

Jenny Macaulay is enjoying retirement in a small coastal town. She is a volunteer tutor at the local Neighbourhood House in drawing, writing and a variety of other programs for seniors. In her spare time she paints and writes, gardens and walks the dog.

Tamsin Martin is a writer, arts administrator and nature enthusiast. She is the winner of the 2015 Grace Marion Wilson Emerging Writers Competition (non-fiction) and is studying Professional Writing and Editing at RMIT. She is writing a memoir about walking alone (and the people she meets along the way).

Janine McGinness-Whyte dislikes constructing biographical notes – she's been writing a long time; won a few, lost a few, published a few. Now living in regional Victoria, with the few.

Paul Mill is an Adelaide-based writer. This is his first published story.

Edie Mitsuda lives and works in the Midwest region of Western Australia.

Port Fairy on the beautiful South West coast has been **Leonie Needham**'s home for almost five years. Local history inspires some of her writing. She plays a variety of hand drums – Irish, African, Middle Eastern – and believes rhythm is essential in both drumming and writing.

Martin Nitschke is an artist that looks at the world around him in the search for something different – perhaps something that cannot be seen by the naked eye. He uses photography as a way to capture this unseen dream.

Aaron Peysack is a Melbourne writer whose work has appeared in *Antipodes* magazine and will be featured in the upcoming editions of *Filling Station* and *Mascara Literary Review*. He is currently putting together a collection of short fiction.

Kristen Roberts' poetry has been published in various journals and anthologies, including *Quadrant, Award Winning Australian Writing, page seventeen* and *The Emma Press Mildly Erotic Anthology*. She has recently begun writing short stories, as some of her poems got too big for their boots.

Anna Ryan-Punch is a Melbourne writer and critic. Her published writing includes work in *Southerly, Overland, Antipodes, The Age, Quadrant, Westerly* and *Island*.

Paul South is a casual animal rescuer and devolving poet. His writing has appeared in journals such as *Cordite, foam:e* and *Offset*. He was the 2013 winner of the Malthouse Theatre Award for Excellence in Creative Arts. Paul has recently moved to Hepburn Springs, and it's unlikely that he will ever come back.

Johanna Stapleton is an emerging writer from Geelong, Victoria. She recently completed a Bachelor of Arts at Deakin University and looks forward to undertaking Honours next year in creative writing.

Ben Walter is a Tasmanian writer. His fiction and poetry have been published widely in Australian journals, including *Overland, Island, Griffith Review, Southerly* and *The Lifted Brow*.

Les Wicks has toured widely and seen publication across twenty countries in eleven languages. His eleventh book of poetry is *Sea of Heartbeak (Unexpected Resilience)* (Puncher & Wattmann, 2013), his twelfth (a Spanish selection) *El Asombrado* (Rochford St, 2015). leswicks.tripod.com/lw.htm.

Rodney Williams' first book was *Rural Dwellings – Gippsland and Beyond* (2008). Ginninderra Press published *A bird-loving man: haiku and tanka* (2013) and *In this dusty rear-view mirror: 55 poems* (2015). Secretary of the Australian Haiku Society, Rodney edited 'Snipe Rising From a Marsh – Birds in Tanka' (Atlas Poetica, USA, 2012).

Bee Williamson is an emerging writer who has self-published plays, a novella and several books of poetry and artwork. She has worked for the last fifteen years as a graphic designer and photographer, graduating from the VCA in 1998. You can see her designs at www.hive.id.au and www.beesboutiquebooks.biz/wordpress.